DELETED

The Mamur Zapt and the Camel of Destruction

Cairo, 1910, and the end of the boom: half-finished buildings everywhere; banks beleaguered; borrowers in trouble, from the poorest land-working Fellahin to the richest land-owning Pashas—not to mention Gareth Owen, the Mamur Zapt, Head of the Cairo Secret Police.

Then one day a civil servant dies at his desk. Was it pressure of work, or some other, nastier, kind of pressure? The whiff of corruption is in the air, with even the Mamur Zapt seen to live beyond his means. Yet he's the one who's supposed to be investigating the affair.

His attempt to do so, aided by such unlikely allies as the local barber, the Grand Mufti, the formidable Widow Shawquat and the monstrous Ali, takes him to the heart of such sinister organizations as the Khedivial Agricultural Society—not at all the same sort of thing as the agricultural societies of places such as Maidenhead (and why do the English go in for such distastefully explicit place names anyway?).

Money speaks louder than words in Cairo and the rich are notoriously tricky. To fight them requires particular skills; skills the Mamur Zapt has in abundance. But Owen will need all his wiles if he is to stop the Camel of Destruction running through the city.

MICHAEL PEARCE

The Mamur Zapt and the Camel of Destruction

THE CRIME CLUB
An Imprint of HarperCollins *Publishers*

First published in Great Britain in 1993
by The Crime Club, an imprint of
HarperCollins Publishers, 77–85 Fulham Palace Road,
Hammersmith, London W6 8JB

9 8 7 6 5 4 3 2 1

Michael Pearce asserts the moral right to be identified
as the author of this work.

A catalogue record for this book is
available from the British Library

ISBN 0 00 232487 3

Photoset in Linotron Baskerville by
Rowland Phototypesetting Ltd
Bury St Edmunds, Suffolk
Printed and bound in Great Britain by
HarperCollins Book Manufacturing, Glasgow

CHAPTER 1

It was, alas, not uncommon for senior members of the Department to nod off in their offices, overcome by their exertions and the heat, so when Abdul Latif stuck his head through the door and observed Osman Fingari he thought nothing of it.

It was, however, decidedly unusual for them to be at their posts after two o'clock, when the city as a whole closed down for its siesta; so when, going round to make sure the shutters were closed, Abdul Latif found him still there at three, he was taken aback.

'It's not like him,' he said in the Orderly Room. 'He's usually away by two.'

'He's usually away by half past eleven,' said one of the other orderlies.

Abdul Latif felt called on to defend his master.

'It's these lunches,' he said.

'That's right. Eat too much, drink too much—'

'Drink too much?' Abdul Latif was shocked. Osman Fingari was, so far as he knew, a strict Moslem.

'He likes his drop.'

Abdul Latif disapproved of this and felt he should bring the conversation to an end.

'We can't leave him there,' he said.

'Why not?'

'It's not proper,' said Abdul Latif firmly. 'Besides, I want to go to the *souk*.'

'Then why not go? He can wake himself up, can't he?'

Unfortunately, this was one thing that Osman Fingari could not do and so it was that the night porter found him still there when he made his rounds at seven o'clock. A cruder individual than Abdul Latif (night porters were paid less than orderlies), and taken by surprise, he said roughly: 'Here, come on, you can't do that!' and shook Osman Fingari by the shoulder.

Whereupon Osman Fingari slid slowly out of his chair and fell to the ground.

'Nasty thing in one of the offices,' said Farquahar in the bar the following lunch-time. 'Chap in Agriculture. Found by the night porter.'

'Heart attack?'

'I expect so.'

In the heat of Cairo such things were not unusual and conversation passed to other topics.

Owen, sitting at a table nearby, heard the remark but did not think it worth registering. People were dying all the time in Cairo. Not in Government offices, of course, or something would have had to be done about it. He had, in any case, more important things on his mind.

'And then the bank manager said to me—'

His companion leaned back wearily.

'Gareth,' he said, 'do you read the newspapers?'

'Of course I read the papers. Damn it, it's my job. Part of it,' he amended.

One of the incidental duties of the Head of Cairo's Secret Police, the Mamur Zapt, was to read the day's press. Actually, he read it twice; before publication, to stop undesirable items from getting in, and after publication, to realize, resignedly, that they had.

'The financial pages?'

'Well, no.'

They consisted, so far as he could see, entirely of numbers; and on the whole numbers were not considered politically inflammatory.

'You should.'

'Cotton prices, contango, that sort of thing? No, thanks.'

'Take cotton prices, for instance. Nothing interesting about them?'

'Absolutely nothing,' said Owen firmly.

'You have not noticed that they are only half what they were a year ago?'

'No.'

Cotton was Agriculture's concern.

'A half, you say? That's rather a fall.'

'It is. And since Egypt depends on cotton, it's reduced the whole national income. By fifteen per cent.'

'Hmm. Well, that does seem a lot. But manageable, manageable.'

'That's what your bank manager's doing. Managing it.'

'Yes, but—'

'It affects the government finances too, of course. In a big way.'

'Fifteen per cent?'

'More.'

'Well, that *is* a bit tough. It explains what they've been doing to my budget. I thought they were just being bloody-minded as usual.'

'A thing like this,' said his companion, who was aide to the Consul-General, 'gives the bloody-minded their chance. The Old Man's hospitality allowance has been cut by half. Half! How I'm going to manage that, I don't know. All these damned visitors! They all expect a free drink, and they measure it in bottles, not glasses.'

'Another one?'

Owen stood up and picked up Paul's glass. Paul glanced at his watch.

'A little one, please. I've got a meeting at three.'

Owen stopped, astonished.

'At *three?*'

The siesta hour, or two, or three, was normally inviolate.

'Yes. It's to do, actually, with the financial pages. Perhaps you should come along.'

'No, thanks. No-o, thanks.'

On the outside wall of the Governorate was a stout wooden box in which from time immemorial the humble folk of Cairo had deposited petitions, denunciations and information which they wished to bring to the attention of the Mamur Zapt.

The Mamur Zapt was no longer the powerful right-hand man of the Sultan he had been in the seventeenth century—indeed, there was no longer a Sultan—but lots of people did not know that and still insisted on writing to him.

They wrote to him about all sorts of things: the price of bread (risen a lot recently); which of the traders was giving short measure (all, but some more than others); the sexual habits of figures prominent in the city (entertaining and quite possibly accurate).

In among the grimy scraps of paper there were often brief, scribbled messages which were of great use to him in his secret service work.

These were the items to which he turned first: but the items he turned to second were the petitions, of which there were usually quite a lot. Many ordinary Cairenes, completely flummoxed by the Egyptian bureaucracy, which was of an Ottoman labyrinthineness, preferred to make use of the more personal mode of address which the Mamur Zapt's box represented.

Owen insisted on handling all petitions himself. Often there was little he could do but he always made sure that, so far as they could be, issues raised were followed up. This was very popular with the ordinary folk of Cairo but less so with the bureaucracy, as Nikos, his Official Clerk, pointed out.

It was one of Nikos's duties to empty the box every day and lay its contents on Owen's desk. He did not like doing this as it meant going out of his office. He preferred to keep his distance from the *hoi polloi*.

That went for the contents of the box, too, which he was quite happy to leave to Owen to deal with. Occasionally, though, Owen needed his help; as this morning.

'Read this. I can't make head nor tail of it. If it's a dowry, I don't want anything to do with it.'

'It's not a dowry,' said Nikos. 'It's a *waqf*.'

A *waqf* was, Owen knew, a religious bequest or endowment. And that was nearly all he knew about it, except that the *waqf* fell under Islamic law (and was therefore nothing to do with him) and was extremely complicated.

'I still don't want anything to do with it.'

Waqfs were quite common. They were a traditional legal arrangement for the giving of alms. A *waqf* was an assignment in perpetuity of the income from a piece of property for charitable purposes, the upkeep of houses for the poor, for example, or the maintenance of mosques or hospitals or schools.

It could also, however, be used for the benefit of the founder's family. The founder could provide for a salary to be paid to a member of his family to act as administrator or stipulate that surplus income be given to his descendants as long as they survived.

Such a system was, of course, open to abuse and over the centuries most possibilities for abuse had been thoroughly explored. From very early days it had been necessary to regulate the system and now, such was the number and scale of *waqfs*, that task was undertaken by an entire Ministry, the Ministry for Religious Endowments.

'Not for me,' said Owen firmly.

'I will tell you about it,' said Nikos, disregarding him.

'It's from a woman, whose husband benefited for many years from a *waqf*. He was a schoolteacher and ran a *kuttub* for small children. It had been in his family for generations.

Anyway, he died and she expected the benefit to pass to their son. It didn't.'

'I thought these things went on forever?'

'So did she. Apparently, though, someone invoked a clause she'd never heard of whereby on the death of her husband the benefit passed to a distant male relative. The relative turned out to be senile and was, she says, tricked into selling the benefit to a rich man who now wants to kick her out.'

'I don't think I can handle this. I'll put her on to somebody in the Ministry.'

'She's already tried them.'

'Well—all right, give me the letter. I'll think about it.'

'There's just one other thing. She says several other people in the neighbourhood have recently lost their benefits in a similar way.'

'The same man?'

'She doesn't say.' Nikos handed back the letter. 'It would be easy to find out. A walk round the neighbourhood. But, then, that's something you like doing, isn't it?'

The phone rang. It was Paul.

'Gareth, the Old Man would like you to take a look at something.'

'Yes?'

'A man died in one of the offices last night.'

'Yes, I think I heard someone say something about it in the bar.'

'Did you, now? It's certainly got around.'

'What's special about it?'

Owen, as Mamur Zapt, or what in England would be known as Head of the Political Branch, did not reckon to concern himself with routine crime, if this was a crime.

'We don't know there *is* anything special about it. It's just that there's been a reaction to it. A political reaction.'

'Ah! Well, isn't that something for you to bother yourself about, not me? I mean, if it's just a heart attack—'

'They're saying it isn't.'

'Who are they?'

'Ali Maher, Abdul Filmi, Al-Nukrashi. And others.'

Owen could understand now. The names were those of prominent politicians. Only one formally belonged to the new Nationalist Party but the others were Nationalist in sympathy and always ready to make the most of any issue which might embarrass the Government.

'But surely the post-mortem—'

'There isn't going to be one. Unless someone says other-wise. A doctor has signed the certificate in the normal way. Natural causes.'

'They why—'

'Ali Maher says it's a fix.'

'What do the family say?'

'They want to get on with it. You'll have to move fast. The body's being buried this evening.'

That was not unusual. Speed was necessary in the heat.

'You want me to order a post-mortem?'

Paul hesitated.

'I want you to take a look at things. Order one only if you think it's really necessary. We don't want this to get bigger than it needs to. That would be playing into Ali Maher's hands.'

Owen, representing the British Administration, went to give his condolences. The family were surprised—they had always known Osman Fingari to be important but hadn't realized he was *that* important—but flattered.

'We knew he'd been doing well in the last year, of course.'

'He's had the house altered a lot.'

'The mandar'ah! New marble entirely.'

'And not the cheapest!'

'Oh, he's done well, all right. But then, he's had to work for it.'

'Yes, never home till late at night.'

'Of course, it took its toll.'

'Well, yes, that was it, of course, wasn't it. In the end he paid the price.'

'You could say he sacrificed himself for his work.'

'Much appreciated,' said Owen. 'Much appreciated.'

They were in the funeral pavilion, which had been erected in the street in front of the house, greatly to the surprise of traffic which had intended to pass by. The tent was crowded, mostly with men in the stiff collar and dark suit and little red pot-like hat, the tarboosh, of the Egyptian civil servant.

'Would it be possible to pay my respects?' Owen asked one of the relatives.

'Of course!'

They pushed their way out of the tent. The street was equally crowded. Apart from onlookers, and as the average Cairene was a great believer in onlooking there were plenty of them, those more intimately involved in the funeral procession were beginning to assemble. There were the blind men, the boys, and the Fikis to chant the suras. There were men with banners and men with torches, for this was evidently going to be a funeral in the old style.

The relative led Owen into the house. From one of the upper floors came the sound of wailing. Owen thought at first that it was the paid mourners but then a door opened and some black-clad women filed down the stairs. The wailing continued up above and he realized that it came from the women of the family.

He followed the relative up the stairs. Outside a door two Fikis were squatting reciting passages from the Koran. The relative pushed open the door and led Owen in.

The body lay in a bier with a rich cashmere shawl draped over it.

Owen advanced and bowed his head. He stood like that for a moment or two and then touched the relative on the arm.

'May I look one last time on the face of someone who was dear to me?'

'Of course!'

But, as he bent over the body, there was really no need to look; the smell by itself was sufficient.

'It was straightforward,' said Owen, 'if you set aside nearly causing a riot, antagonizing the Ulama, provoking the Kadi, irritating the Khedive and raising uproar in the National Assembly. Not to mention upsetting a rather nice old couple still in a state of shock after losing their son.'

'I'm sorry about that,' said Paul. 'The others I can live with.'

'And was it worth it, I ask myself? So he did take poison; where does that get us? Does it matter if he took poison? That's his business, isn't it?'

'Well, not entirely. *Why* did he take poison? That's the question they're asking.'

'How do I know? Girlfriend, boyfriend, personal problems, fit of depression, overwork—yes, and while we're on that subject, can I just mention that I was up all last night trying to get the quarter to calm down.'

'You poor chap! And can I just mention that I myself was up half the night trying to sort out something that was much bigger.'

'What was that?'

'The stupidity of bankers.'

'Heavens, you'll never be able to do anything about *that*. My bank manager—never mind my bank manager, what about this chap commiting suicide, what are we going to do about him? And, incidentally—' a ray of hope gleamed—'why am *I* doing anything about it at all? It's nothing to do with me. Suicides, murders—that's the Parquet's business, surely?'

In Egypt responsibility for investigating a suspected crime did not lie with the police but with the Department of Prosecutions of the Ministry of Justice, the Parquet, as it was known.

'The Parquet will have to be involved, certainly. It's a crime, of sorts, and they'll have to be notified. They'll check on the circumstances, etc., etc., and make a fine pig's ear of it, no doubt, but their part of it really is straightforward. No, no, they can be left to get on with that bit. It's the other bit—'

'What other bit?' asked Owen. 'It sounds as if it's just a question of managing the Assembly and that's something you and the Old Man can do, surely? You're doing it all the time!'

Paul did not reply at once. Owen hoped he was having second thoughts. He wasn't.

'I think you'd better stay with it, Gareth,' he said.

'Doing what?'

'Asking yourself why Osman Fingari committed suicide. And why Ali Maher and Co. are so interested.'

There was, then, going to be not one investigation but two. This was, actually, nothing out of the ordinary, for Egypt was a country of parallel processes. There was, for example, not one legal system but four, each with its own courts. Knowledgeable criminals played off one court against another. If they were very knowledgeable, or rich enough to afford a good lawyer, they could often escape conviction altogether.

A similar parallelity could be observed in Government, though here there were only two Governments and not four. One, the formal one, was that of the Khedive; the other, the real one, was that of the British, who had come into Egypt twenty years before to help the Khedive sort out his finances and were still helping. Every Minister, Egyptian, had an Adviser, British, right beside him. The Prime Minister did not; but found it politic to draw abundantly on the wisdom of the Consul-General before adopting a course of action. The system worked surprisingly well. From the British point of view, of course.

Mohammed Fehmi, the Parquet lawyer appointed to handle the case, was an experienced hand. The following morning he called on Owen in his office.

'Coffee?'

'Please.'

'Mazboot?'

Mohammed Fehmi, like most Egyptians, preferred it sweetened.

'About this case now—'

'Sad.'

'Oh yes. Very sad. But straightforward, I would think, wouldn't you?'

Mohammed Fehmi's alert brown eyes watched Owen sharply across the cup.

'Oh yes. Straightforward, I would say.'

'I was wondering—' Mohammed Fehmi sipped his coffee again—'I was wondering—the nature of the Mamur Zapt's interest?'

'General. Oh, very general,' Owen assured him, 'I wouldn't be thinking of taking, um, an active interest—'

'I would always welcome a colleague—'

'Oh no. Quite unnecessary, I assure you. Every confidence—'

Mohammed Fehmi looked slightly puzzled.

'Then, why, may I ask—?'

'Am I involving myself at all?' Owen saw no reason why he should not speak the truth. 'It's not so much the case itself—that I leave entirely to you—as the possible reaction to it. Politically, I mean.'

'A *fonctionnaire?* Civil servant?'

Mohammed Fehmi was still puzzled. However, he shrugged his shoulders. This was evidently political in some strange way and politics was not for him. He was not one of the Parquet's high fliers.

He had picked up, however, that Owen was leaving the conduct of the investigation to him, and visibly relaxed.

'After all,' he said, 'a simple suicide!'

'Exactly.'

'The post-mortem—quite definite.'

'Oh yes.'

'I'll just have to find out where he got it from. And why he took it, of course.'

'Up to a point.'

'Oh yes,' Mohammed Fehmi assured him swiftly. 'Only up to a point. Otherwise you find yourself into personal matters, family matters, even social matters, that are best left alone.'

'Quite so.'

'No,' said Mohammed Fehmi, finishing his cup and sucking up the last mixture of coffee grounds and sugar, the sweet and the bitter, the taste of Egypt, 'no, the only puzzling thing about it is why the doctor signed the certificate in the first place.'

Owen called the doctor in. He was a small, shabby man with worried eyes and a lined, anxious face.

'How did you come to miss it?'

'I didn't miss it.'

'You wrote the certificate knowingly?'

The doctor shrugged.

'You know, of course, what this means?'

The doctor shrugged again. 'You do it all the time,' he said quietly.

'Sign certificates you know to be false?'

'It spares the family.'

'You know why we have the system of certification?'

'Of course. To prevent abuses.'

Egypt was a country of many abuses.

'And you still thought you would sign the certificate?'

'The parents are old. He was their only son. The shock of that was enough without the other.'

'The other?'

'Suicide.'

'Are you sure it was suicide?'

'What else could it be?'

'The Under-Secretary,' said Nikos. 'The Ministry of Agriculture.'

Owen picked up the phone.

'Captain Owen? I understand you're handling the Fingari case?'

'Well, of course, the Parquet—'

'Quite so, quite so. But—I understand you're taking an interest?'

'Ye-es, in a general way.'

'Quite so. I was wondering—the circumstances—a bit unfortunate, you know.'

'Yes?'

'The Office. The Ministry.'

'I don't quite—'

'Bad for the Department. A bit of a reflection, you know.'

'Well, yes, but—'

'I was wondering—just wondering—if it could be moved. Out of the office, I mean.'

'Surely it *has* been moved?' said Owen, startled. 'It was taken for post-mortem. And before that, the funeral. I saw it myself—'

'No, no. I don't mean that. Not the body. The—the incident, rather.'

'I don't quite follow—'

'Moved. Out of the Ministry altogether. Somewhere else.

Into the street, perhaps. Or at any rate another Ministry. Public Works, perhaps.'

'Finance?'

'Yes. No, on second thoughts. The follow-up could be, well, unfortunate. No, no. Public Works would be better.'

'Well, yes, but—'

'You will? Oh, thank you.'

'An apéritif, perhaps?'

He had met them, as they had suggested, in the bar at the Hotel Continentale. There was an Egyptian, who must be Abdul Khalil, a Greek, Zokosis, presumably, and someone harder to place but definitely a Levantine of sorts, who would be Kifouri.

The waiter brought the drinks: sweet Cyprus wine for Zokosis and Kifouri, a dry sherry for Owen and coffee for Abdul Khalil.

'As I mentioned over the phone, Captain Owen, we're businessmen who have quite a lot of dealings with Government Departments. I think you'll find that Mr Stephens would be prepared to vouch for us—' Stephens was the Adviser at the Ministry of Finance—'and I think it is a mark of our standing that the Minister invited us to join the Board. I mention this so that you will know we are *bona fide* and also that we are not the sort of men who would want to waste the time of a busy man like yourself.'

Owen bowed acknowledgement.

'In any case, our concern is, what shall I say, marginal, peripheral, which is why we thought it best to meet informally rather than call on you at your office.'

Owen muttered something suitably non-committal.

'You are, we understand, taking an interest in a recent sad case of suicide. A man in one of the Departments.'

'Yes.'

'Well, now, we naturally wouldn't wish to interfere in any way, believe me, in any way, with your conduct of the investigation—that would be quite improper—and our interest is, as I have said, marginal. However, we knew Mr Fingari and quite recently have been having a number of dealings with him—'

'Dealings?'

'A businessman's way of talking. Conversations, rather. Yes, conversations. Mr Fingari, you see, represented the Ministry on the Board. And naturally, in view of recent developments—'

'Yes, recent developments,' echoed the others.

'That, actually, is why we wanted to have an informal word with you. You see, negotiations are at a critical stage—'

'And it's important to carry the community with us. The business community, that is.'

'And with confidence so low—'

'It is really a very inopportune moment for him to die.'

'Most difficult.'

'Now if only he could have died a day or two later—'

'You don't think that could be arranged by any chance, Captain Owen? After all, it makes no real difference. He's dead anyway, isn't he?'

'The family—' Owen began.

'Leave that to us. I'm sure that could be arranged. We'll talk to them, Captain Owen.'

'But—'

'Look at it like this; it's actually giving the poor chap a few extra days of life. Don't be hard-hearted, Captain Owen. Don't deny him that! Think of the poor fellow, think of his family—'

'You want me to alter the date of his death?'

'Well, that would be most kind of you, Captain Owen. Most kind.'

'It's the family, you see.'

'Distressed, naturally.'

'It is a very respectable family,' said Ali Hazurat earnestly. 'Otherwise Mr Hemdi would not wish his daughter to marry into it.'

'But—'

'The arrangements were all made. The wedding contract was about to be signed. My nephew was looking forward—'

'A dowry?'

'Considerable. It was a great opportunity for my nephew. And now, alas—'

'But surely the wedding can go ahead? After a suitable period, of course. Your nephew was not *that* closely related to Osman Fingari.'

'It reflects on the family, you see. It's making Mr Hemdi think again.'

'Well, I'm sorry about that, but—'

'It's the shame, you see. Suicide! No one will want to marry into a family with suicides.'

'I'm afraid I really don't see what I can do—'

'Couldn't you,' pleaded Ali Hazwat, 'just call it something else? An accident, perhaps?'

'He took prussic acid.'

'By mistake! Couldn't it be by mistake? He thought it was something else. The wrong bottle—'

'Well, at least there's going to be no doubt about the circumstances,' said Paul.

'No?'

CHAPTER 2

'Alone? Certainly not!' Mr Istaq was shocked.

'I do not wish to trouble Mr Fingari, you see.'

'Well, no, there's been enough trouble as it is.'

'And he's very frail, so I thought—'

'Well, yes, but—alone! What can you be thinking of, effendi? She is a decent Muslim girl.'

'It was just that in the circumstances—'

'Why do you want to see her, anyway, effendi? What can a woman know? Why not ask me? I will do what I can to help you.'

'Well, thank you, it is very kind of you, Mr Istaq. But then, you see, you would not be able to help me in quite the same way. After all, though a relative, you did not actually live in the house and therefore would not know—'

'Yes, but alone! With a man! No, really, effendi—'

Mr Istaq, hot, bothered and worried in equal proportions, took some time to be persuaded. He was, when all was said and done, the relative who had shown Owen the body and felt that he bore some responsibility for the consequences.

But then, he was also the closest and most senior male relative and, given old Mr Fingari's frailty, it all devolved on him anyway. He was a simple journeyman tailor and all this was a bit much for him.

He knew, however, what was proper. And it was not proper to let his niece talk to strange men. Aisha was inclined to be headstrong, anyway. His brother had always given her too much scope. That was all very well, things were not, perhaps, what they used to be, but who would want to marry a woman used to having her own way? And it was likely to be him, Istaq, who would be left with the problem of marrying her off.

In the end a compromise was reached. Owen was allowed to interview her but in Mr Istaq's presence.

Owen had always known this was the most likely outcome. It was customary in Egypt for female witnesses to be interviewed through their father or husband or a near male relative. He had, however, hoped to avoid it in this case.

The girl appeared, heavily veiled and dressed from head

to foot in decent, shapeless black. All that could be seen of her was her eyes, which were suitably cast down.

'Miss Fingari, I am sorry to trouble you further in such sad circumstances but there are one or two things I would like to ask you.'

The girl moved slightly and Mr Istaq cleared his throat.

'You saw your brother every day, of course?'

Mr Istaq looked at Aisha, hesitated and then reluctantly admitted that this was so.

'Had you noticed a change of spirits in him lately?'

'No,' said Mr Istaq confidently.

'Had he seemed at all worried?'

'No.'

'Perhaps a little depressed occasionally?'

'No.'

The girl had not yet spoken.

'I ask,' said Owen, 'because I am wondering what could have brought him to this sad state of mind?'

He put it as a question and then waited, looking inquiringly directly at the girl.

She did not reply. Mr Istaq, not quite sure how to respond, muttered uncertainly: 'No sad state'.

'Had he ever talked to you about problems at work?'

'Certainly not!' said Mr Istaq, shocked.

'Or problems not at work. Not at home, of course, but in his private life?'

'No,' said Mr Istaq firmly.

'I wonder,' said Owen, 'if there had been any changes lately in his way of life?'

'No,' said Mr Istaq.

'But that is not true, Miss Fingari,' said Owen, still addressing himself to the girl although she had not yet spoken. 'Everyone knows that there had been changes in his way of life. He had had a lot done to the house, for a start.'

'No changes!' snapped Mr Istaq, caught off balance.

'But there had been!' said Owen, wide-eyed. 'The man-
dar'ah—new marble! And I think the better of him for it.
So often people rise in the world and forget their family.
But was Osman Fingari like that?'

'No,' said the girl firmly.

'No,' echoed Mr Istaq.

'Everyone says he loved his parents.'

'He did,' said the girl.

'He did,' said Mr Istaq.

'But they were old, Miss Fingari, and he would not have
wanted to trouble them. So did he discuss his problems
with you, I wonder?'

'No,' said Mr Istaq.

The girl said nothing. Her eyes, though, were now raised
and she was looking at Owen directly.

'You see, when men are brought to such a desperate
pass, when they are in a state so desperate that they can
contemplate a thing like this, it is often because they feel
themselves quite alone. Did Osman Fingari feel himself so
alone, I ask myself.'

The girl's eyes filled with tears.

'Was there no one he could turn to? No one in the whole
wide world?'

'Why do you ask these things,' the girl suddenly burst
out. 'What business is it of yours? What do you care about
my brother?'

'Aisha!' cried Mr Istaq, scandalized. 'Be quiet, girl! You
have said enough, more than enough!'

Things were worse even than he had feared. The girl had
no idea how to behave.

'You do not address your elders like that!'

The girl dissolved in a flood of tears.

Both men were at a loss.

'Now, now!' said Mr Istaq, chiding but at bottom kind-
hearted. He had overdone it. The girl wasn't used to being

corrected. 'It's all right! I think we had better stop,' he said
to Owen.

'Of course!' Owen could have kicked himself. 'I am sorry,
Miss Fingari. I have no wish to distress you. I have to ask
these things. You see, sometimes it is something inside a
person that makes them do a thing like this and sometimes
it is something outside—'

'I think we had better stop,' said Mr Istaq.

Owen, dissatisfied with himself, stopped for a coffee round
the corner. He was sitting at a table sipping it when a small
boy touched him on the arm. Automatically he felt in his
pocket.

'No, no, effendi!' protested the small boy. 'Not that! At
least, not just that. Perhaps afterwards—when you have
heard my message.'

'You have a message for me?'

'Yes, effendi, though I must say, I'm a bit surprised at
it, because she's not been that way before.'

'Just a minute,' said Owen. 'Who sent you?'

'Aisha.'

'Miss Fingari?'

'That's right. Only we call her Aisha.'

'What's the message?'

The little boy reflected. 'I ought to bargain with you—'

'Twenty milliemes?'

'Say, twenty-five.'

'Twenty-five it is.'

'Right, then. She wants to see you. Not with her uncle.'

'Does she say where?'

'She does. But, effendi, she does not know much about
this sort of thing and I do not think that what she proposes
is a good idea. She says she will go to the *souk* and you can
meet her on the way. But, effendi, that is not the way to
do it.'

'What is the way to do it?'

'For that, effendi, I would need the full half piastre.'

'A fee which fits your talents. For a suitable place no doubt I could find such a sum, exorbitant though it be.'

'In this world one has to strike hard bargains,' said the small boy sententiously.

'Yes, indeed. What do you suggest?'

'There is a ruined house nearby—'

'Is it decent enough for Miss Fingari?'

Places like that were used as lavatories.

'No, but there is a doorway where you would not be seen. It is not very comfortable for your purpose—'

'My purpose is only conversation.'

'Well, of course, it's early days yet—'

The boy led him to the spot. It was a place where two or three tenement buildings had crumbled down together. This was not unusual in Cairo. Houses were often made of sun-dried mud brick and in the rains sometimes dissolved.

The boy picked a way through the rubble, squeezed through a gap between two crumbling walls and brought Owen to an archway set deep below ground level in what remained of the side of a building. It had, perhaps, once led into a cellar.

'Wait there!' he said.

A few moments later, Aisha's veiled form appeared in the gap and stood before the archway uncertainly.

'Miss Fingari—'

'I shouldn't have come here like this. Ali is horrible. Go away, Ali! Mind you go right away! It's not what you think.'

She came forward determinedly and stepped into the archway.

'I shouldn't be doing this. But I had to see you.'

'It is about Osman?'

'Yes.'

Under the archway it was dark. Instinctively, she retreated deeper into the shadow. He could not see her eyes but he could tell from the position of her body that she was looking up at him.

'You hurt me,' she said, a little shakily, 'when you said he felt alone.'

'I don't know that. It was just—'

'It was true. Oh, it was true. It must have been true. I tried! But—'

'You must not blame yourself, Miss Fingari. It is not always possible to break through.'

'No,' she said. 'I should have tried harder. I became impatient. When he came home—' She broke off.

'When he came home—?'

'Sometimes he had been drinking. Oh, it's not such a great fault, I see that now; but it was so different, so—so unexpected. He had always been—he had always behaved properly—'

'He was a strict Moslem?'

'Not strict, but—but he did what he should. Until—'

'Recently?'

'Yes.'

'You saw a change in him?'

'Yes.'

'What sort of change, Miss Fingari?'

'He became—not disorderly, but not so ordered. He would come home late. He never used to do that. Now he did it often. He wouldn't say where he had been—'

'You asked him?'

'Yes. We were close. We had been close. He would talk to me when he wouldn't— He didn't always feel he *could*— talk to my parents.'

'What did he talk about, Miss Fingari?'

'Oh, nothing much. This goes back a long time. To when he was at school. If something had gone wrong during the day, if someone had been unkind to him, he would run home and pour it all out to me. I was his big sister and— and I remained so even after he started work.'

'He still talked to you?'

'Yes. Perhaps even more so. Our parents were growing older. They did not always understand the sort of things he was doing at work—'

'But you did?'

'No!' She laughed. 'How could I? A woman? Shut up in the house all day. All I knew was the family and the *souk*. But I had friends, other girls, and they talked about their brothers and I—I learned something, I suppose. Anyway, he felt he could talk to me.'

'And then he stopped talking to you? When was this?'

'It was not—not suddenly, not like that. It just—built up over time.'

'But when did it start? When did you first become aware that you could not talk to him as you used to?'

'I   I don't know. Recently. The last few months.'

'Since he joined the Board?'

'No. Yes, I suppose,' she said, surprised. 'But, effendi, he was not like that. It was not because he became proud. Oh, he was proud of being appointed to the Board, he was very proud of it—and so were we all—but it wasn't—that wasn't the reason.'

'He did change, though?'

'Not because of that.'

'Why are you so sure?'

'Because I know him. And—and because he did talk to me about that, about the people he met—they were very famous people, effendi, even I had heard of them—about the places he used to go to. No, it was not that, it was— afterwards.'

'Afterwards?'

'About the time he started coming home later.'

'That was some time after he had joined the Board?'

'Yes.'

'Have you any idea, Miss Fingari, why that was? Why did he start coming home late?'

'He—he was meeting someone. I—I thought it was a woman and teased him. But it wasn't. He said it wasn't. And then—'

'Yes?'

'That was when he started to come home smelling of drink. I knew then that it was not a woman, that it was someone who was bad for him. I was angry with him, I told him he must not see them, but he said—he said he had to see them—'

'Had to?'

'Yes. He said it was business and I said what sort of business was it if it was in the evening and he came home smelling of drink after it and he became angry and said I did not understand. And after that he would not speak with me.'

She began to sob.

'If I had not been so fierce, perhaps he would have spoken to me. Perhaps I would have been able to help him, save him—'

'You must not blame yourself, Miss Fingari.'

'But I do blame myself!' she said, sobbing. 'I do blame myself. You were right when you spoke of him being alone. He was alone, and he would not have been if I—'

'You did what you could, Miss Fingari.'

'No, not what I could!'

There was a little spasm of sobbing in the shadows. He moved towards her uncertainly, intending to comfort her, but then she stepped forward herself and seized him by the arms.

'But if I am to blame,' she hissed, 'so are they! They brought him to this! You said there was something outside himself. Someone. There was!'

'Miss Fingari, these may just have been friends—'

'No. He was different after he had been with them. He began to be different all the time. There was a change, oh yes, there was a change!'

'You said he was more lax in his behaviour—'

'No, not lax. Not just lax. Different. They were bad men, Owen effendi. They changed him. He had always been a good man, a good son, a good brother . . .'

She began to weep steadily.

'Effendi, you are too rough with her,' said a voice from outside the archway. 'Didn't I tell you she doesn't know about this sort of thing?'

The sobbing stopped abruptly. There was a sharp intake of breath.

'Ali, you are disgusting!' said Aisha, and stalked out into the sunlight.

'First, it was the *kuttub*. Then it was the hospital. Then it was the Place for Old People. I tell you, they're determined to get you one way or another. Next thing, it will be the cemetery!'

'Next thing it will be the mosque. That comes before the cemetery.'

'It already is the mosque. Have you talked to Sayid ben Ali Abd'al Shaward lately?'

'Not him too! I tell you, they're determined to get us one way or another. The little we've got, they want to take away! That's how it always is for the poor man.'

A general mutter of agreement ran round the circle squatting round the barber's chair.

'Abd el-Rahim is not a poor man!' someone objected.

'I'm not talking about Abd el-Rahim,' said the barber, flourishing his scissors. 'I'm talking about *us!*'

'Watch it!' said the man in the chair, flinching as the blades flashed past his ear.

The barber ignored him and turned to address the assembly.

'Don't you see? We're the ones who are going to lose out. They'll take the *kuttub* away. Well, you'll say, I don't mind that; my children are grown up. But then, what about the hospital? What about the Place for Old People? You will mind that one day!'

'What about the mosque?' muttered someone.

'You can always go to another one,' said someone else.

'Yes, but that's my point,' said the barber. 'You can always go to another one. Your children can go to another *kuttub*, you can drag your aching bones to another hospital or your old bones to another Place for Old People, but they'll be somewhere *else!*'

'Are you going to cut my hair or not?' asked the man in the chair.

The barber turned back to him hurriedly.

'What will become of the neighbourhood,' he asked over his shoulder, 'if they take all our amenities away?'

'It's going downhill anyway,' said someone. 'It's been going downhill ever since those Sudanis moved in.'

'It will go downhill a lot faster if there isn't a *kuttub* and a hospital,' said the barber, declining to be diverted. The Sudanis were customers of his.

'The Shawquats have always had that *kuttub*,' said someone ruminatively.

'And done very well out of it,' said someone else sceptically.

'Yes, but it's terrible to take it away just when they need it, now that the old man's died.'

'They've still got a piastre or two, I'll bet. I shan't be shedding any tears for them.'

'It still doesn't seem right. They've always had it.'

The barber swung round excitedly.

'*We've* always had it. The *waqfs* were set up to benefit *us*. And now they're being taken away. All right, the Shawquats have done well out of it, and so has Sayid ben Ali Abd'al Shawad; but *we're* the ones who are going to lose!'

'He's cut me!' shouted the man in the chair.

'It's nothing! Just a scratch!'

'I'm bleeding!'

'He moved! Didn't he move?' the barber appealed to the crowd.

'I didn't move! I haven't moved at all!'

'My God, he's dead!' said a caustic voice from the back of the crowd.

Owen eased himself out of the circle. With his dark Welsh colouring and in a tarboosh he looked like any other Levantine effendi: a clerk, perhaps, in the Ministry of Agriculture.

'It's a bit of the Camels, old boy,' said Barclay, of Public Works, that evening at the club.

'Camels?' said Owen, bewildered. So far as he had been aware, they had been talking about the destructiveness of road development in an urban environment.

'Well, Camel at least. Have you heard of the Camel of Destruction? No? It's a figure from legend, a sort of Apocalyptic Beast. At the beginning of the world, or soon thereafter, it ran amok and threatened to destroy everything. And if you've ever seen a camel going wild among a lot of tents you'll know that that means *everything*, but everything!'

'We've got past the tent stage now, Barclay,' said someone superciliously.

'Yes, but we haven't done away with the Camel of Destruction,' said Barclay. 'Oh no, my goodness we haven't. Just look around you! Beautiful buildings being pulled down, monsters being put up.'

'I'd assumed that was all your doing, Barclay,' said the supercilious one. 'You're responsible for planning, aren't you?'

'I may be responsible,' said Barclay, 'but there's nothing I can do about it.'

'In Cairo,' said someone else, 'money is the only thing that talks.'

'Well, of course, it's a complete racket,' said Barclay.

'They have to submit plans but then if we turn them down, they can proceed all the same. There's nothing we can do.'

'Don't you have to give planning permission?'

'No. Take the Hotel Vista, for instance. You've seen that big block on the corner of the Sharia El Mustaquat? They sent us the plans. Anyone with half an eye could see they wouldn't do. The foundations were unstable, the retaining walls—well! We condemned it on grounds of public safety. The next thing we heard, it was going straight ahead.'

There was a general shaking of heads.

'Mud for mortar. No wonder they come down as fast as they go up!'

'And there are still plenty going up!'

'Not as many as there were.'

In the boom of recent years a frenzy of building had overtaken the city. Rows of houses were pulled down; great blocks were run up. And then, when they were only half way up, and neither up nor down, the money had run out. With the general tightening of credit, projects were abandoned all over Cairo, leaving the city looking like one huge derelict building site.

'There are a few still going ahead,' said Barclay. 'One or two of the bigger projects where they've borrowed a lot of money and the banks are pressing them and unless they get something back quick they're sunk.'

'Anyone buying up land for the next round yet?' asked Owen. 'When it all starts up again?'

'No need to do that,' said Barclay. 'There's land a-plenty. Why do you ask?'

'Just wondering,' said Owen.

Later in the evening he found himself standing next to Barclay at the bar.

'Heard anything about any development in the Derb Aiah area?' he asked.

'No,' said Barclay, 'and I wouldn't want to. It's a nice old part—do you know it? Lots of nice old houses. *Rabas,* not Mameluke—it's not rich enough for that. Really old, sixteenth-century, I would say, some of them. Some fine public buildings, too, only they're very small and tucked away among the houses so it's easy to miss them. A mediæval hospital, tiny, but, well, I'd say unique. Take you over there, if you like, and show you.'

'I'd like that,' said Owen. 'Next week perhaps?'

'Friday? Fine! It'd be a pleasure.'

Passing Barclay's table later in the evening, he caught Barclay looking up at him meditatively.

'I say, old chap, you've got me worried. There isn't anything going on in the Derb Aiah area, is there? I'd hate that part to be spoiled.'

'I'm not sure.'

'The only thing I can think of,' said Barclay, 'is that someone might be being very smart and thinking a long way ahead.'

'What might they be thinking?'

'They might be thinking about the new road there's talk of on the east side of the city.'

'What new road is this?'

'It's no more than a gleam in the eye, really. But it's the Khedive's eye.'

'There are lots of gleams in his eye,' said Owen dismissively.

The Khedive's ambition to emulate the great predecessors who had done so much to modernize Egypt was well known.

'But the money always runs out. Yes, I know,' said Barclay.

'It'll never happen,' said Owen confidently.

'Perhaps someone thinks that this time it will.'

'Yes, but even if it does . . . I mean, that would be over on the east side of the city, or so you said. It wouldn't affect the Derb Aiah.'

'It might. That's why I said it might be someone who

was looking ahead. They might be thinking that the next road after that would be one thrown across the north of the city to join the Clot Bey. Right through the Derb Aiah.'

'But that—that's so speculative!'

'That's how speculators make their money. By speculating.'

'It's— It's—'

'It's unlikely. Yes, I know. It'll probably never happen. But you did ask.'

'Yes, I did. And thanks for telling me. Though I don't think, in fact—'

'I hope I'm wrong. Let's drink to me being wrong. I wouldn't want to see the Derb Aiah turned into a building site.'

'Cheers!'

A thought struck him as he put down his glass.

'That other road, the one on the east side of the city: what line would it take?'

'It would drop south from the Bab el Futuh and come out in the Rumeleh, roughly at the Bab el Azab.'

'But that would go straight through the Old City!'

'Yes.'

'It would cause a riot!'

Barclay looked into his beer.

'Ah yes, I dare say. But that would be something for you, old boy, wouldn't it?'

'It's all right,' said Paul soothingly. 'It will never happen. The money won't be there. It never has been, it never will be, and it certainly isn't there at the moment. And, talking of money—' he glanced at his watch—'I've got to go to another of these blessed meetings. You wouldn't like to come along, would you?'

'No,' said Owen.

'You could sit at the back. It would be good preparation.'

'Preparation? What for?'

'Sitting at the front. That's the first item on the agenda for today, you see.'

'The Mamur Zapt? About time too!' said Abdul Aziz Filmi.

The meeting was being held at the Consulate-General, an indication of its importance, as were the people present. Apart from Abdul Aziz, who was the sole representative of the Opposition, there were half a dozen prominent politicians. Owen realized later that they were the senior mentors of the Assembly's Finance Committee.

There was the Minister there, his Adviser, British, so it must be important, the Governor of the Bank of Egypt, British, one or two foreign bankers and Paul, representing the Consul-General.

'I don't agree with you,' said the Minister sharply. 'And isn't it anticipating the agenda? I thought we were going to discuss this.'

'Captain Owen is not attending as a participant member,' said Paul smoothly. 'He has observer status only.'

'That's precisely the trouble,' said Abdul Filmi. 'This committee's full of observers. No one is actually *doing* anything.'

'There, I think, you're failing to anticipate the agenda, Mr Filmi,' said Paul. 'Shall we begin?'

The subject of the meeting was the current difficulties of the Agricultural Bank. The Bank had been set up a few years before to address the problems of Egypt's cotton-producing fellahin, or peasants. Chief among these was their chronic indebtedness.

They borrowed to buy the land in the first place; they borrowed to buy seed and fertilizer; and they borrowed in order to live when their returns fell short of their costs. The trouble was that they borrowed from local moneylenders at rates of interest so high as to make it virtually impossible for them ever to repay.

The Agricultural Bank was intended to cut through all

this. It lent only to Egyptians (the foreign bankers were not too happy about this), it lent only to fellahin and not to rich landowners (the Minister was not too happy about this) and it lent at low rates of interest (none of the bankers were happy about this). However, it worked.

For a time. But then international cotton prices fell, the boom came to an end, interest rates rose and everyone was in trouble. The Bank was in trouble.

'Over-lent,' said one of the foreign bankers.

'Under-secured,' said another.

And so, only more so, were the fellahin. A few weeks before, the Bank had started foreclosing on its loans.

'Outrageous!' fumed Filmi.

'Devastating!' murmured the politicians.

But fortunately the fellahin did not have votes.

'A financial disaster!' said the British, who were there, after all, to help the Egyptians avoid financial disasters.

The Bank, in their view, was underfunded. This was not the view of the foreign bankers, however. Nor was it the view of Abdul Aziz Filmi. The money was there, all right. Or should have been there.

'Where has it gone?'

'Costs of the recession,' said the Governor of the Bank of Egypt.

'Administrative expenses,' said the Adviser.

'Inefficiency and waste,' said the overseas bankers.

'Corruption,' said Abdul Aziz Filmi.

CHAPTER 3

'And what exactly was the nature of Mr Fingari's work?' asked Owen.

The Under-Secretary, behind his desk, began to shuffle papers.

'His work? Oh yes. Well, very important. This is an important Department, Captain Owen. New, but important. Our budget does not really reflect . . . Of course, you can't do much with £20,000 (Egyptian). Not if you have to cover the whole country. And not with something like Agriculture. But it's an important Department.'

'I see.'

'We do our best. Of course, with the Khedivial Agricultural Society—'

'The Khedivial Agricultural Society?'

'Yes. A very vigorous body. Set up by the Khedive himself a few years ago. With the help of some of your own distinguished compatriots.'

'The Society comes under your Department, does it?'

'Oh no, no. Quite independent. Private, you might say. And vigorous, very vigorous.'

'It promotes discussion, I take it?'

'Oh yes. Very ardent discussion, yes. And also—'

'Yes?'

'It sells.'

'It engages in business on its own account?'

'Yes. It sells seed. It has an arrangement with the Agricultural Bank.'

'I see.'

'Yes. And—and services, too. It sells services. Veterinary services, pest control . . . Excellent services, Captain Owen. Of course, we don't quite have the money ourselves . . .'

'What is the relationship between the Society and your Department?'

'Oh, good. Very good.'

'Yes, but what does the Department do that the Society does not do?'

The Under-Secretary regarded him thoughtfully.

'Manure,' he said.

'The Department supplies manure?'

'No, no. The Society does that. Too. That's another service they offer. And fertilizer.'

'But then what does the Department do?'

'Paperwork,' said the Under-Secretary. 'Yes, paperwork.'

'I see. And that's what Mr Fingari was doing?'

'Yes.'

'May I see his office?'

The Under-Secretary summoned a minion to conduct Owen along the corridor but then, unusually, accompanied Owen himself. On the way they acquired several other minions.

The office was of the sort common in the Ministries; high-ceilinged, because of the heat, dark because of the heavy shutters, and oddly green because of the light filtering through the green slats of the shutters. From the ceiling was suspended a huge fan.

Owen glanced at the papers on the desk.

'All to do with the Agricultural Bank,' he said.

'Well, of course; he was the Department's representative.'

'Was there anything special that he was engaged with?'

'No,' said the Under-Secretary, 'no, I don't think so.'

'I was under the impression that there was.'

'No. I don't think so.'

The Minister and the minions departed, leaving Owen alone in Osman Fingari's office. He went through the desk systematically and then began on the filing cabinets. They were half empty.

He went back to Osman Fingari's desk and sat down. A turbaned head appeared round the door.

'Would the Effendi care for some coffee?' asked Abdul Latif.

The Effendi certainly would.

Abdul Latif disappeared and then came back with a tray

on which was set a small brass cup and a large brass coffee-pot.

'This was how Fingari effendi liked it.'

Owen lifted the lid of the pot. Turkish. He poured some out.

'Sugar in the right-hand drawer,' said Abdul Latif.

'I see you are a man who knows his Effendi's ways.'

'I did his office,' said Abdul Latif proudly.

The dramatic events of the past week had seen a great rise in his status in the orderly room.

'And very well, too,' said Owen, looking around.

'I like to keep on top of things,' said Abdul Latif modestly, pouncing on a spot of coffee on the tray with his duster.

'And do you also bring the mail?'

'I do.'

'What a weight to carry!' said Owen, shaking his head.

'A weight to carry?' said Abdul Latif, surprised.

'But what did he actually do?' asked Owen.

He was talking now to one of Osman Fingari's colleagues.

'The Bank—'

'*All* his time?'

'Preparation—'

'*All* his time?'

The man capitulated.

'Perhaps he wasn't very busy,' he admitted.

'Are you all like that? Not very busy?'

'We should be so lucky!' said the man bitterly. 'There are only twenty of us and we have to cover the whole country. They've got more in the Agricultural Society!'

'Then how is it that Fingari wasn't?'

'Perhaps—he's joined us only recently, perhaps he's not had time to pick things up—'

'How recently?'

'Six months. Before that he was at Public Works.'

'He came to you from Public Works?'

'Yes. He was brought in specially. So that he could represent us on the Bank. To be fair, he had the background—'

'Banking?'

'Control of public expenditure.'

'And none of you have that background?'

'Not to the same extent. Public Works is large. We are—small.'

'What did he do with the rest of his time? When he wasn't working on the Bank?'

'I don't know. None of us know. He kept himself to himself.'

'Did anyone work with him?'

'No. His work was, as I have said, very specialized.'

'So you wouldn't know anything about these negotiations he's been engaged in?'

'Negotiations? I didn't know he had been engaged in any. What sort of negotiations?'

'I'm like you: don't know anything about it.'

'He's certainly been going out a lot lately,' said the man thoughtfully. 'But we thought—you know, lunch and all that sort of thing—'

'You don't know any of the people he used to meet?'

The man shook his head.

'We didn't really like to ask him. Thought they might be people he'd worked with when he was at Public Works.'

'No names?'

'They'd be in his desk diary. We're supposed to record—'

'It doesn't seem to be here,' said Owen, searching.

'Isn't it? It ought to be. Ya Abdul!'

Abdul Latif appeared in the doorway.

'Fingari effendi's Green Book: have you seen it?'

'It should be on the desk,' said Abdul Latif, coming into the room.

*

The Ministry of Agriculture was, as it happened, in the same building as the Ministry of Public Works, occupying part of a corridor on the top floor at the back, which indicated, in the subtle way of the Civil Service, its status as a *parvenu*.

The building was in the Ministerial Quarter, the Kasr-el-Dubara, which was itself in the same state of incompleteness as the rest of Cairo. Half of it consisted of grubbed up gardens and abandoned foundations, a memento of the recent land-boom, in which the part on the river bank was to have been developed as a fashionable residential area.

The other half of it had already been developed with imposing new Government buildings, set out in French-style ornamental parks with formal flowerbeds and cool promenades of trees.

Owen had intended taking to the promenades but as he came round the corner of the building he saw in front of him the handsome, if rather stolid, edifice of the Ministry of Religious Endowments. Since he was in the neighbourhood . . .

'I would like to check the details of a *waqf* I am interested in,' he told the clerk at the Reception desk inside 'It's in the Derb Aiah area.'

The clerk, a Nikos in embryo, looked at Owen sniffily.

'We do not classify them by areas,' he said.

'How do you classify them?'

'By names.'

'Shawquat.'

'What sort of name is that?'

'It's the name of the beneficiary.'

'Ah, we don't classify by the names of beneficiaries. We classify by the name of the original endower.'

'Mightn't he be named Shawquat, too?'

'He might; but then, again, he might not.'

'Try under Shawquat,' said Owen.

The clerk took his time.

'There are several Shawquats.'

'Fine. I'll look at them all.'

'The files would be too heavy to bring.'

'I'll look at them where they are.'

Reluctantly, the clerk took him into a back room, very large, occupying the whole of one floor of the vast building.

'Thank you. How are they organized?'

'In files.'

Owen considered whether to pick the clerk up, shake him and drop him. But this was not one of the Ministries with an English Adviser, it was a Ministry which, in view of the nature of its business, history mixed with religion, the English thought it politic to leave alone. So he didn't.

'Arranged alphabetically by the initial letter of the name?'

'Of course.'

The clerk went off. As he disappeared behind the stacks Owen heard a voice say softly in Arabic:

'Is that courteous?'

'It is only a foreign effendi—'

'Then that is worse. For in that case you are representing not just the Ministry but also our country: and what will the foreign effendi think of a country whose servants behave as you have just been doing?'

'I said nothing—'

'I heard what you said. And now I will tell you what you will do. You will go round and you will collect all the files that the effendi needs and you will take them to him.'

'I—' began the clerk, but then stopped abruptly.

He began to bring Owen files at speed.

Owen went round the stack to thank his benefactor. He found a young Egyptian, smartly dressed, not in the usual dark suit of the office effendi, but in a light, white, French-style cotton suit and a red tie exactly chosen to go with his red tarboosh.

He was sitting at a table reading one of the files but

looked up politely as Owen approached. His eyes opened wide in surprise and he jumped up.

'*Mon cher ami!*'

'Mahmoud!'

'I didn't realize—'

They embraced warmly in the Arab fashion.

'But why,' demanded Mahmoud, disengaging himself, 'did you put up with him?'

'Well, I thought, this is a special Ministry—'

'But why did you think that?'

'The religious connection—'

'But you mustn't think that! It is just a Ministry like any other. You mustn't expect less than you would from other Departments. That is to insult it.'

'It's not that, exactly—'

'But this is important! If you do not apply the same standards, is it because you think this is only an Egyptian Department, it's not a proper one?'

'No, no. Certainly not! Look, it's not worth bothering about.'

'But it is, it is,' cried Mahmoud excitedly. 'You put up with it because you say, "They are only Egyptians, you can't expect anything better;" and that is bad, that is to wrong us, to insult us—'

'I don't do anything of the sort   '

'It is to apply a double standard, one for the English, another for the Egyptians!'

'Nonsense!'

'Tell me,' said Mahmoud fiercely, 'would you expect the same service if you were in England?'

It was a long time since Owen had been in England. He considered the matter honestly.

'Yes,' he said firmly.

'Yes?'

Mahmoud stopped, astonished.

'They're the same the whole world over.'

'They are?'

'They are.'

'Well . . .' said Mahmoud, deflating. 'Well . . . All the same,' he shot out as the unfortunate clerk scurried past, 'the service here needs improving!'

They were old friends and had, indeed, worked together on several important cases. Mahmoud was a lawyer, a rising star of the Parquet.

'What are you doing here?' asked Owen.

'Working up a case,' said Mahmoud. 'It starts tomorrow.'

'I didn't know you were an expert on *waqfs*.'

'I'm not. That's why I'm going over it again before I get in court.'

'Can I get some free legal advice? No, I'll tell you what, I'll pay for it. I'll take you out to lunch.'

'You don't need to pay for it,' said Mahmoud, 'but lunch would be a pleasure.'

They agreed to meet at one and for the rest of the morning Owen worked on the files the clerk had brought him, after which he was little the wiser.

'It *is* complicated,' Mahmoud admitted over lunch, 'but basically what you want to know is: can a *waqf* be set aside?'

'That's right.'

'On what grounds?'

'Well, you tell me. Public interest?'

Mahmoud shook his head.

'Not a chance. There *is* an issue of public interest, since the endowment was established for the benefit of local children. But if the endowment has merely been transferred, the issue does not arise.'

'If it's a developer, he's going to close down the school.'

'You'd have to wait until it was clear that was what he was going to do.'

'It would be too late, then. He'd have demolished the building.'

'It wouldn't matter anyway because he could always say he was going to open another school somewhere else in the neighbourhood.'

'What about the argument that the relative didn't know what he was doing when he sold the benefit? The Widow Shawquat said he was senile.'

'She'd have to be able to prove that.'

'I don't know that she'd be very good at proving anything. Not if it came to a real legal wrangle with lawyers. The other side would be able to afford good lawyers and she wouldn't.'

'I'd do it myself,' said Mahmoud, 'only I'm going to be tied up for at least two months. This is a big case.'

'Oh heavens, no; I wasn't dreaming of involving you to that extent. In fact, I wasn't really thinking of involving the Widow Shawquat if I didn't have to. I was wondering if I could appeal myself.'

'As Mamur Zapt?' Mahmoud frowned. 'I wouldn't do that if I were you. The Ministry is nationalist, not in my way but in a different way. They would be prejudiced from the start.'

'What do I do, then? Someone's got to formally appeal, presumably?'

'Yes. But it ought to be someone who would impress the Ministry of Religious Endowments. Someone preferably of religious weight. And that, *cher ami*,' said Mahmoud drily, 'is not you.'

The Agricultural Bank occupied the first and second floors of a large modern building in the Ismailiya Quarter. The ground floor was occupied by a furrier's, which in the climate of Egypt might appear to err on the optimistic side. The Ismailiya, however, was the fashionable European quarter and its purchasers were thinking more of France than they were of Egypt.

Owen asked about access to the Bank.

'We don't deal directly with the public,' said the clerk to the Board loftily.

He was another Copt, like Nikos. The original inhabitants of the city, before even the Arabs, the Copts seemed to take to administration naturally and settled in the Ministries like water finding its own level.

The Arabs couldn't understand it at all. They thought they had defeated them and now here they were being governed by them! It was another of the little things that didn't help the popular attitude towards the Civil Service.

'How do you deal with them, then?' asked Owen.

'We lay down policy.'

'I thought you made grants to fellahin?'

'We do that through the *omda*.' The village headman.

'And you don't go out to the villages yourselves?'

'I believe some people do.'

He brought Owen minutes of the Board's meetings and papers recently considered.

'Self-explanatory, I think.'

Owen detained him.

'The thing I'm trying to establish is Mr Fingari's exact role.'

'He represented the Ministry.'

'I know. What did he do?'

'He expressed the Ministry's viewpoint.'

'Which was?'

The clerk gestured towards the papers.

'It's all in the minutes,' he said.

A Greek, expensively dressed and with an air of seniority, came through the door. Owen recognized him. It was Zokosis, one of the businessmen who had invited him to meet them at the Hotel Continentale. He shook hands.

'I hope Petros has been helping you?'

'We have some way to go.'

'Ah!' He sat down. 'Try me.'

'Thank you. I'm trying to establish what Fingari actually *did*.'

The Greek laughed. 'Good question,' he said. 'At least, I think so. I wonder what any of them do. Well, look, all I can do is tell you what he did for us. He attended Board meetings once a month. Meetings usually occupy the whole morning.'

'And in between?'

'Well, of course, there would be papers to read. Possibly he even drafted one or two papers. Although off-hand I can't . . . I'll get Petros to check.'

'Anything else?'

'I really can't recall . . .'

'You know, Mr Zokosis, you surprise me. You gave me the impression at the Continentale that his work was important.'

'Did I? A businessman's way of talking, perhaps.'

'You wanted me to change the date of his death.'

'Not quite as crudely as that, I hope. But certainly his death was inconvenient to us. You see, we were just negotiating—we thought we *had* negotiated, in fact—an important arrangement with the Ministry and we didn't want to go through all that again.'

'The arrangement was to do with what?'

'An injection of funds. Well, no, perhaps that is to go too far. Let us say, the Ministry was going to underwrite a credit arrangement on our part.'

'You were going to borrow money and the Ministry was going to guarantee it?'

'That's the general idea, yes.'

'And Fingari's role in this?'

'He represented the Ministry in the negotiations.'

'And was also on your board.'

'Yes.' Zokosis smiled. 'It's all right, Captain Owen. There is nothing underhand about it. The operations of the Bank are so crucial to the agricultural sector that it makes sense for the Department to be party to our deliberations. We requested the appointment because we wished to be open about our thinking.'

'Yes, I'm sure. But that doesn't seem to me to be quite the same thing as entering into a financial relationship.'

'One is a natural extension of the other. Especially in the present situation,' said Zokosis seriously, 'with the whole agricultural sector in danger of collapsing. You are, of course, aware—?'

'One has only to look at cotton prices,' said Owen. 'However, I am still wondering about Fingari's role in the matter. Did he have the power to authorize the arrangement himself?'

'Heavens, no! It had to go right the way up.'

'And did?'

Zokosis smiled. 'I can see you're still unconvinced. Would you like to have a word with our Chairman?'

'You're not the Chairman?'

'Oh no. I'm merely Chief Executive.'

He led Owen along the corridor, knocked on a door and entered.

'Mr Singleby Stokes', he said.

'Hello, old man,' said the white-haired, white-moustached man sitting behind the desk. 'Don't think we've met.' He rose and shook hands. 'Not been in the country long, of course.'

'Four years,' said Owen.

'Ah well. Been here for forty years, myself. Started in currants in Alexandria. One thing led to another and here I am today.'

'A banker?'

'And other things. Plenty of irons in the fire. Safe pair of hands, that's what I am. And if you're like that, a lot of things come your way.'

'Captain Owen was wondering about our arrangement

with the Ministry. He wants to know if it's bona fide,' said
Zokosis.

'Bona? About as bona as anything is in Egypt, old boy.
Absolutely copper-bottomed. Talked to the C-G myself.'

'You've talked to the Consul-General?'

'See him regularly, old boy. Tuesday evening, regular as
clockwork. Get the old tables out. Whist. Bridge. Don't
go there to talk business, mind. Bad form, that. But the
occasional word. Keep him posted.'

'I see,' said Owen.

'You see,' said Zokosis.

CHAPTER 4

'I myself,' said the Under-Secretary impressively, 'ordered
it to be locked the moment I came in. And it has been kept
locked ever since.'

Abdul Latif held up his hand.

'The Parquet—' he began.

'Well, of course,' said the Under Secretary brusquely, 'it
was opened for the Parquet. But then it was locked again.
Mr Fehmi explicitly asked that it should be. And I, of
course, was willing to conform.'

'Mr Fingari almost certainly had some appointments,'
said Owen. 'Might not someone, the clerk in the office,
perhaps, have come in to collect the diary so that they could
cancel his appointments?'

The Under-Secretary turned to the Chief Clerk. 'Well?'

The Chief Clerk shook his head. 'Mr Fingari handled his
appointments himself,' he said. 'We had nothing to do with
them.'

'And you didn't think,' said the Under-Secretary sternly,
'that when he died it might fall on you—?'

The Chief Clerk studied the ground.

'No, effendi. Besides, you had expressly said the room was to be kept locked.'

'And you never went in?' asked Owen.

'Never, effendi,' said the Chief Clerk positively.

'The office was kept locked,' said the Under-Secretary firmly. 'Nothing in it was touched—'

Abdul Latif twitched.

'Yes, I know,' said the Under-Secretary impatiently. 'The Parquet came to go through it. And then the Mamur Zapt came. THEY DON'T COUNT! No—one—else—went in. The room was left untouched.'

Abdul Latif cleared his throat.

'Abdul Latif,' began the Under-Secretary, with rising fury.

'Excuse me, effendi. But that is not so.'

'Not so?'

'No, effendi. The fact is, effendi,' said Abdul Latif apologetically, 'I went in. Well, I had to, didn't I?' he appealed to Owen. 'If you don't do the room every day, the sand comes in through the shutters and covers everything. You wouldn't want to look at the papers, would you, if they were all sandy? So I came in and dusted.'

'How did you get in, if the room was locked?'

'I have a separate key. I have a key to all the rooms. This is my floor,' said Abdul Latif proudly.

'Separate key!' moaned the Under-Secretary.

'And where do you keep the key when you are not using it?' asked Owen.

Abdul Latif looked bashful.

'I keep it next to my genitals, effendi.'

'What?' almost screamed the Under-Secretary.

'Yes, effendi.'

Abdul Latif lifted the skirts of his galabeah and tugged out a massive bunch of keys from his woollen underpants.

'Some keep them next to their heart, lest they get stolen. But I keep them next to my genitals, for that is a more sensitive place, is it not? I would know at once if a hand—'

'Thank you, Abdul Latif,' said the Under-Secretary. 'That is more than enough.'

Left alone, Owen went through the office once more. He had been through it already this morning and had little hope of finding the diary, but he wanted to make sure. Afterwards, he sat down in Osman Fingari's chair and looked at Osman Fingari's desk.

The top was neatly arranged, with in-tray to the right, out-tray to the left, inkwell and brass pen-box directly in front. No doubt Abdul Latif had rearranged everything, but then he probably did that every morning and it looked as if Osman Fingari had been content to accept his orderliness.

There was almost certainly a regular place for his diary. Abdul Latif, the other day, had looked straight at a spot on the desk and pronounced the diary missing. Its absence did not appear to be explicable in terms of ordinary office processes. It was beginning to look as if it had not just been mislaid.

There was a knock on the door and Abdul Latif stuck his head in.

'Would the effendi like some coffee?'

He returned a little later carrying the tray Owen had seen before.

'This is how Mr Fingari used to like it,' he said, placing the tray on the desk in front of Owen.

'I see you know how to look after your master, Abdul Latif.'

'Well—' said Abdul Latif modestly.

He poured Owen come coffee and stood anxiously by while Owen tested it.

'Delicious!' said Owen, smacking his lips with extra smack to show appreciation.

Abdul Latif, relieved, poured him some more.

'It's good coffee,' he said, 'but not everyone likes this sort. They all bring their own little boxes, you know. This comes from Mr Fingari's, but I'm sure he wouldn't mind.'

'Creatures of habit, are they?'

'Never change a thing. But at least you know where you are with them.'

'And Mr Fingari was like that, too, was he?'

'Well, he was. Or seemed to be. And then suddenly he was always going out. Especially at lunch-time. Mind you,' said Abdul Latif loyally, 'it wasn't the way Musa says it was. He didn't go out every day. And he certainly didn't go at half past eleven!'

'Popping out for some coffee? You surprise me, with such excellent—' Owen took another sip.

'No, no, no. And it wasn't drink, either, despite what Musa says. No, it was business. He used to have these lunches. And I know it was business because once he forgot to take some papers with him and he sent back for me to bring them to him.'

'He was in a café, was he?'

'Yes, effendi. But it was not one of your ordinary cafés, such as you or I might go to, or, perhaps, you might go to. It was a place where rich men of business go and talk about important things.'

'Really? Do I know it, I wonder?'

'It is in the Sharia es Shakhain, not far from here.'

'I think I know it. But are there not several restaurants in that street?'

'I don't remember. But this was one is where Greeks go.'

'Ah!'

'Very splendid it was. There was an orderly at the door in a beautiful uniform, and he said: "This is not the place for one like you." And I said: "I have some papers for Fingari effendi." And he said: "Give them to me." And I said: "No, for I was told to put them into my master's hand." So he let me in and I saw that it was sumptuous.'

'Did you see the people he was with?'

'I did not mark them, effendi. I—I was overcome.'

'Nevertheless, they couldn't have done their business without you,' Owen pointed out.

'True,' said Abdul Latif, struck. 'True.'

'And, plainly, it was as you say and not as Musa says: business was being done.'

'Musa is like a pair of bellows,' said Abdul Latif. 'All wind.'

He picked up the tray and balanced it one-handed while with the other he dabbed at a spot on the desk and straightened out the pen-box.

'You are a man of method, Abdul Latif,' said Owen, watching him, 'and therefore I am surprised that you cannot tell me when the diary went missing. You dusted the papers every day. Did you not dust the diary, too?'

'Yes, effendi, I did,' said Abdul Latif. 'It was there on the desk. Until the Parquet came.'

Owen took Zeinab to the restaurant for lunch. She was quite pleased about this as she had spent the morning in the Ismailiya Quarter shopping.

'Greek would be all right,' she said, 'as long as it's not full of boring businessmen.'

It was full of boring businessmen but by this time, having traipsed around the Ismailiya all morning and then having come by stuffy arabeah to the Sharia es Sakhaim, she was prepared to settle.

She was the only woman in the restaurant. Even in the modern European quarters it was rare for women to mix with men in public. In advanced upper-class circles, where the culture was heavily French, it was increasingly common for them to appear at private parties. But that was at home and among friends. It was the exceptional woman, or the foreigner, who dared risk opprobrium by appearing in public.

Zeinab was quite prepared to play the foreigner when it suited her. Speaking French as naturally as she spoke Arabic, thinking French, and accompanied by someone who was manifestly foreign, she found this easy; and quite relished the assertion of her independence.

Even so, in deference to local susceptibilities, she dressed in black and wore a veil, although her attire owed more to Paris than it did to Islam. Like many upper-class Cairene women, she conceded as little as she could to local fashion and tilted as much as she dared in the direction of Paris, from where she acquired the majority of her dresses, at prices which made Owen flinch.

He flinched now when she showed him her spoils of the morning. Not that he had to pay for them; Zeinab received an allowance from her bewildered father, a wealthy, Europeanized Pasha. But Owen had lately begun to think seriously of marriage and was wondering now how Zeinab's tastes squared with his income.

'Stunning!' he said, as she showed him the handbag she had just bought; though he was thinking less of the handbag itself than of its price.

'Nice, isn't it? Of course, it won't do for everyday wear. Nor for special occasions. But I'm keeping my eyes open.'

The restaurant was already full, so full that a latecomer, a Greek, like the majority of the clients, had to have a table brought for him.

'Ah well,' said the newcomer, as the *patron* tried to squeeze him in, 'at least you're in the right business. You know what they say: serve food to Greeks and you'll never be short of customers.'

'The trouble is,' said the *patron*, calling for the waiter to give the table a perfunctory wipe, 'the customers are short of money.'

'You too?' said the Greek, picking up the menu. 'You know, that's just what I'm finding.'

'Everyone's finding it. There just isn't the money about. An apéritif?'

'Why not? Better not have anything after that, though. They count every millieme these days.'

The *patron* poured him a glass of sweet Greek wine and took one himself.

'Work for the Government?'

'If only I did!'

The *patron* laughed.

'Yes,' he said, 'they never seem short of money, do they? I get quite a few of them in here, you know. From the Ministries. It's a good steady trade. It's that that keeps me going, really. Of course, there aren't many of them in today, it being Friday.'

'As a matter of fact,' said the Greek, 'I was hoping to meet one of them. A Mr Fingari. He told me he often came here.'

The *patron* looked round. 'Not here today,' he said.

'You know him?'

'Been here quite often lately.'

'He was going to introduce me to some of his friends.'

'He's often here with friends. But I don't think any of them are here today.'

'You'd recognize them, would you? Look, I've got a job over here and I'll be popping in most days for a bit. Perhaps you could point them out to me if you see them?'

'Sure,' said the *patron*, making way for the waiter.

'Satisfied?' asked Zeinab.

'It'll do,' said Owen.

'He's claimed for lunch every day this week,' said Nikos indignantly.

'That's all right.'

'I hope it is all right,' said Nikos. 'We're running out of money under that heading.'

'Journal transfer some in from another account.'

'Are you crazy? We'd have to ask Finance for permission first. And that would direct their attention to it. Is that what you want? Overspent the hospitality allocation?'

'Perhaps you'd better put it under some other heading.'

Nikos threw down his pen in exasperation.

'You can't do that! There are rules in this business, you know. They put you in prison for something like that.'

'It's only a little—'

'It's the principle. That's the whole point. You've got to stick to principles. The same principles. Everyone!'

'Surely no one would notice—'

Nikos breathed heavily.

'They have a whole Section which devotes itself to noticing. It's called Audit.'

He turned back to his papers and thrust out a hand. 'Receipts!' he commanded.

The man standing in front of his desk put his hand in his pocket and fished out a crumpled piece of paper.

'I've got discipline,' he said.

He was a Greek, the one, in fact, who had come to the restaurant late and talked to the *patron*. His name was Georgiades and he was one of Owen's agents.

'You!' said Nikos witheringly. 'You're the one who's led him into it.'

Owen was roused to protest. 'I'm just trying to do my job,' he said. 'All this stuff gets in the way.'

'You're the people who introduced it,' Nikos pointed out.

One of the first things Cromer had done when he was appointed Consul-General had been to introduce modern accounting procedures into the chaotic, and corrupt, system of Egypt's finances. It was commonly regarded—outside Egypt—as his greatest triumph.

Nikos had taken to the new procedures—they were, after all, bureaucratic procedures—like a duck to water and was jealous in their defence.

'He needs to be able to have a few more lunches,' said Owen. 'It's important.'

'Quite right,' said Georgiades. 'Rosa's been cutting down on the food lately. She says I'm overweight.'

'Well, all right,' said Nikos. 'It's just that if he eats them now, he won't be able to eat them later.'

'Hard times,' said Georgiades, as he followed Owen out of the office, 'and harder to come. That's what they all say. You know, I don't understand this financial stuff at all. What's gone wrong? We were doing all right, weren't we?'

'We were doing too all right, apparently. That seems to be the root of the problem.'

'I'm a child in these things,' Georgiades confided. 'Rosa does all the sums in our household. What a head that girl has got! It comes from the old woman, you know, her grandmother. Sharp as a knife! Looks after it all. I stay right out of it.'

'A good thing you married her,' said Owen.

'*He* married *her*?' said Nikos from his desk. '*She* married *him*.'

Barclay was as good as his word and showed Owen round the Derb Aiah district. It was a warren of narrow, mediæval streets to the north of the Ezbekiyeh Gardens, lying between the newer European quarter to the west and the Old City to the east.

At first sight it was unpromising since it seemed to be an area of *rabas*, tenements consisting of one or two sleeping- or living-rooms, a kitchen and latrine (but not a bathroom; you went outside to wash). Many of them were built above shops.

They were easy to pick out because they tended to be built at an angle to the street; that is, instead of there being a flat wall above the shop, there was a sort of triangular street corner with windows looking both ways, windows without glass, of course, just fretted woodwork which gave passage to the air and allowed the women inside to observe without being observed. In Cairo you always felt as if you were being watched; and you usually were.

'This street, old boy.'

Half way along the street, tucked in behind the *rabas*, were some marvellous old Mameluke houses. The box-like windows of each storey projected further and further across the street so that at the top they almost touched the windows opposite. The structures rose like the fortress of a Spanish galleon.

'Look at the woodwork!' breathed Barclay. 'There's no one who can do that today. Once that goes—'

They went down the tiniest of alleyways and came out in a small square. At first it looked a very ordinary little square with nothing to mark it out except a rather plain flight of mosque steps which appeared to lead up to a blank wall.

But at the top of the steps there was an open passage, at the other end of which there was something blue and shining. They went down the passage and came out in a courtyard. In the centre of the courtyard was a blue tower. It flashed and shone in the sunlight, sparkling like a turquoise.

'It's the tiles, you see,' said Barclay.

The tower was faced with thousands of tiny blue tiles which caught and reflected the sunlight like the facets of a precious stone.

They went inside. The tower was, Owen realized, a small Dervish mosque. It was fitted out with fine, soft carpets and beautiful glass mosque lamps. From the dome, painted blue to match the tiles outside, hung a cage of fretted meshrebiya woodwork, with a canopy roof like a Turkish fountain and lots of Moslem prayers hanging from it.

They came out and walked round the outside. At the back of the tower there was some scaffolding and some men were at work repairing the tiles.

'It's being restored,' said Barclay. 'By the *Waqfs*.'

'*Waqfs?*'

'Ministry of.'

'I thought they just administered the endowments?'

'They do. Upkeep is part of the administration.'

A young man came round the corner carrying a piece of broken tile. He recognized Barclay and smiled at him.

'This is Selim,' said Barclay. 'He does quite a bit of work for us.'

'When it's there,' said the young man, shaking hands. 'At the moment there's more with the *Waqfs*.'

'Do you specialize in restoration?' asked Owen.

'I'd like to. But there really isn't enough work of that sort. Especially now. It's one of the things that get cut.'

'He's done some lovely work,' said Barclay. 'I'll show you one day.'

'Thanks. I'd like to see it.'

They shook hands and moved on.

'Good chap,' said Barclay. 'A bit political, but he knows his job.'

At the top of the steps they turned and looked back.

'A gem!' said Barclay. 'Pity if that got in the way of a developer.'

The Widow Shawquat, impressed but slightly flustered at so exalted a response to the letter she had placed in the Mamur Zapt's box, was prepared to receive him. Mindful of proprieties, however, she could do so only in the presence of a suitable male and it took a little while to find him; especially as, equally mindful of what was her business and not that of her neighbours, she went to some pains to choose one who was deaf.

Eventually, though, Owen was seated on a low, moth-eaten divan with a brazier in front of him on which a brass pot of coffee was warming.

'The Mamur Zapt, eh,' said the Widow, wriggling with pleasure, 'in my house!'

'Be quiet, woman!' shouted the old man. 'Men speak first!'

The Widow, behind her veil, gave him a look but subsided.

The old man, conscious, too, of proprieties, clapped his hands.

'Coffee!' he bawled. 'Coffee for the Effendi!'

An old woman scuttled in and poured Owen some coffee in a small brass cup. Owen sipped it dutifully and praised it copiously. It was quite some time before they were able to get down to business.

'Please tell the Widow Shawquat that when the Mamur Zapt read her letter he was deeply concerned.'

'The Effendi was deeply concerned,' the old man told the Widow.

The Widow's eyes flashed impatiently but she said nothing.

'I cannot promise to do anything for her since this is really the business of the Ministry of *Waqfs.*'

'This is not woman's business,' shouted the old man.

Owen thought he saw a distinct bridle on the part of the Widow Shawquat but ploughed on.

'I will do what I can, however. It would help if she gave me some more details. The *waqf,* for instance—'

'What?' said the old man.

'The *waqf,*' shouted the Widow.

'What? Oh, *waqf.*'

'It was in the name of your husband, naturally.'

'My husband's family—be quiet, you, the Effendi can't wait all day—the Shawquats. It went back to his great-great-grandfather's time. It's always been in the family. I wouldn't have married him if it hadn't been. What was Ali Shawquat to me, a rich woman, with my own property—'

'What property?' asked the old man suddenly.

'My uncle's shop—'

'That wasn't your property!'

'It would have been—'

'The *waqf*,' said Owen.

'It was the *waqf*, you see. Without that he wouldn't have been anything. Oh, a nice enough man but weak—oh, so weak! You wouldn't believe it! Mind you, it's not always bad when a man is like that, it means you can get on with things in your own way. But then something comes along like this—my son's just the same, he's not going to get anywhere without his mother behind him—'

'The *waqf* was in the name of the Shawquats and entitled them to what?'

'The *kuttub*. It's in the fountain-house in the El Merdani.'

'Your husband received a salary as headmaster?'

'Yes. Not much, but more than a man like him could earn anywhere else. And more than my layabout of a son could earn, though in his case it's his own fault, he's intelligent enough, anyone can see that—'

'And then, when your husband died—?'

'Some man comes along in a smart suit and a tarboosh and tells us it doesn't belong to us any more!'

'His name?'

'I don't know. He probably hasn't got a name. He probably hasn't got a father, not one that would acknowledge him—'

'Yes, yes. Can you give me the name of the relative it passed to?'

'Mungali Shawquat. Rashid Mungali Shawquat,' she spat out. 'But he's not really a relative, he's so far removed ... and no relative would behave like that, not even a Shawquat. Of course, you may say it's not his fault, the old fool is senile, but then whose fault is it, I ask? And he's not so senile as all that, he got some cash for it, I'll be bound. Of course, all the Shawquats are a bit simple—'

'And now it's in the hands of—?'

'Mr Adli Nazwas. That was his name.'

'Have you got his address?'

'Address?' The Widow stopped in mid-flow.

'Were you sent a letter?'

'A letter? People like me don't get sent letters. His man came round, this man in the tarboosh, and said: "Now you've got to get out. Be gone. By next Friday!"'

'So the school is already closed?'

'Closed?' said the Widow Shawquat indignantly. 'Certainly not! My son's along there. He doesn't know anything but he'll do as a teacher. He was at school himself, wasn't he? Well then, he can do it.'

'But I thought you said—'

'It'll close,' said the Widow Shawquat with determination, 'when they throw us out. And that won't be so simple. I've told my son, Abdul, I said, if the men come, just send for me. I'll send them off with their tails between their legs, you see if I don't! That's right, isn't it, Mustapha?' she appealed to the old man.

The old man had, however, fallen into one of the cat-naps of the aged.

The Widow shrugged.

'But, effendi,' she said, turning back to Owen, 'what if they send the police?'

Owen thought it probable that the redoubtable widow would send them packing too. Aloud, however, he said sternly: 'The law must be obeyed.'

'But what if it's unjust?'

'There are proper ways of seeking redress.'

'That's just what I said!' cried the Widow, gratified. 'My very words! I said, we're going to have to set about this in the proper way. So I put a letter in your box.'

'Yes, well—'

The Widow Shawquat eased her bulky frame forward to the edge of the divan and dropped on to her knees in the traditional posture of the suppliant.

'You can stop them, effendi! You are the Protector of the Poor, the Hope of the Unfortunate—'

Her voice rose into a sing-song.

'No, no!' said Owen hastily.

'The Righter of Wrongs! The Sword of the People!'

'Please stop.'

'The Mamur Zapt is the All-Powerful!'

'Not any more. Look, it's all changed.'

'They are strong and we are weak but you will stand between us!'

'Look—'

She clutched at his jacket, which was not quite as service-able for the purpose as a galabeah, and kissed it.

'You are our Father and Mother—'

'All right, all right. I'll do what I can.'

The Widow stopped in mid-wail.

'You will help us?'

'Yes, but—'

The Widow started to raise her voice in a pæan of grati-tude, but checked on seeing Owen's face.

'I will do what I can,' said Owen. 'But these things are not straightforward.'

'I know that,' said the Widow, easing herself back up on to the divan. 'Adli Naswas is tricky and deceitful. So I said, let us go to someone who is tricky, too. And so, effendi, I turned to you.'

'Thank you.'

'I went first,' said the Widow, 'to the Sheikh of our mosque. But he is without guile in these matters. All he could say was that he would speak to the Mufti '

'The Mufti!'

The Mufti was the chief authority on religious law. One thing Owen could do without was for this to become a religious dispute.

'But what good will that do?' asked the Widow bitterly. 'The Mufti will speak to the Ministry and then what? They will do nothing. For Adli Naswas has already spoken to them. And money speaks more loudly than words in our city.'

She dug the old man heavily in the ribs.

'Here, you, wake up! A fine thing! Supposed to be my protector and falls asleep! Why,' said the Widow Shawquat with relish, 'I might have been raped four times!'

CHAPTER 5

'This is the fourth lunch he's had at our expense this week!' said Nikos indignantly. 'This way financial disaster lies.'

'I'm following up a lead,' protested Georgiades. 'It's the only one we've got.'

'You're following it up with too much enthusiasm,' said Nikos.

'I'm like that,' said Georgiades.

'You're like that when you think you're getting something for nothing.'

Georgiades shrugged. 'A man's entitled to a free lunch occasionally.'

'There is no such thing as a free lunch. Someone has to pay for it. I do.'

'Who is this "I"?' Georgiades asked Owen. 'Has he taken over running the Department or something?'

'I am the voice of Lord Cromer,' Nikos announced grandly.

'He left Egypt four years ago.'

'His spirit lives.'

Georgiades turned to Owen. 'You're not going to let him get away with this?'

'Four is a bit much.'

'Just when I was getting somewhere,' said Georgiades dejectedly.

'Where are you getting?'

Georgiades helped himself to a drink of water from the large earthenware pitcher which, as in all Cairo offices, stood in the window to be cooled by the air which came through the shutters.

'Is this OK?' he asked Nikos, with the glass in his hand. 'Or does Lord Cromer object to people having free drinks, too?'

Nikos disdained to reply.

'Are you getting anywhere?'

Georgiades perched himself on the end of Nikos's desk.

'I've got three names,' he said. 'I'm following them up.'

'Anything interesting?'

'Two are from the Agricultural Bank.'

'Directors? Or officials?'

'Officials. Working lunches, my friend the *patron* says.'

'You've no idea what they were working on?'

'Not yet. I am, as it happens, having lunch with one of them tomorrow.'

'Another!' cried Nikos.

'You want me to stop?' Georgiades asked Owen.

'You'd better go ahead. But try to cut them down,' advised Owen.

'It might be nothing. A lot of papers. Sounds like the civil service to me. The third man might be more interesting, though.'

'Name?'

'Jabir. Jabir Sabry. Young. Effendi. Suit, of course. But no papers.'

'Have you talked to him?'

'No. I need to know more about him before I do that. With the people from the Agricultural Bank it was OK. I could be a businessman talking to businessmen. They understand that sort of thing. But I don't even know that this bloke is a businessman.'

'Did they drink? Aisha said that Fingari had started

coming home the worse for wear. He'd been mixing with
a bad lot, she said.'

'They drank. They all drank.'

'Yes, but people from a bank wouldn't count as a bad
lot, not to her.'

'It was lunch. They'd do proper drinking separately.'

'You might try and find out about that.'

'Yes. Actually,' said Georgiades, 'there's something you
might be able to find out.'

'Yes?'

'Better than me. Apparently, this man Jabir was an old
friend of Fingari's. At least, that's the impression the *patron*
got, hearing them talking. College, or possibly, even,
school.'

'You want me to ask Aisha about it?'

'Could you?'

'I'll try. The trouble is, it's always difficult getting to talk
to women on their own. I'll have a go, anyway.'

But, as he approached the Fingaris' house, he was having
second thoughts. If he went to the door and asked to see
Miss Fingari, he would certainly be refused. The uncle,
Istaq, would probably not be there, and he had had enough
difficulty with him last time. Aisha wouldn't see him on
her own, not publicly, that was; and he was loath to involve
the parents.

He walked on past the house, turned and walked round
the square, thinking. And then, seeing a convenient table,
he sat down in a little Arab café and ordered coffee.

An irrelevant thought struck him. Should he pay for this
coffee himself or should he charge it to expenses? Normally,
he would pay for it himself, thinking that drinking coffee
was strictly in the course of the day's duties and disliking
filling in forms over piffling details. But should he be taking
this relaxed view?

He wouldn't be here if it wasn't for his duties and thinking was work, wasn't it? If he didn't claim for it, he was, in fact, giving money to the Government. Did he want to give money to the Government? He did not.

Besides, it was all very well for a bachelor to take a relaxed view about money. But if he was thinking of getting married, especially to Zeinab, relaxing about money was the last thing he could afford.

Unfortunately, if he was getting married to Zeinab, cutting down on the coffee bills wouldn't help much, either.

He moved his chair as a water-cart went past spraying out water behind to damp down the dust in the streets. The main thoroughfares were done first thing in the morning; they only got to little squares like this much later.

As always, the cart was followed by a crowd of urchins dancing in and out of the spray. The sight of them gave him an idea.

He beckoned them over to him.

'Do you know a boy named Ali?'

'We know lots of boys named Ali.'

'He lives around here somewhere.'

'You were here the other day, weren't you, effendi?'

'Yes, he saw Aisha.'

'Do you want to see Aisha again, effendi? I could fix that up. You don't need Ali.'

'Yes, you do.'

It was the original, authentic Ali, materializing from nowhere.

'Don't listen to him, effendi. He is a lying, cheating scoundrel. Besides, Aisha doesn't like him.'

'She doesn't like you much either, Ali.'

'I am useful to her,' declared Ali in a lordly fashion. 'She trusts me. The Effendi does too.'

Owen distributed some milliemes and Ali drove his rivals away.

'Now, effendi, what can I do for you?'

'I'd like to see Aisha.'

'Difficult, difficult. She is guarded as by the beast of a hundred eyes.'

'Who's guarding her?'

Ali disregarded this question.

'It could be managed; though at a price.'

He named a figure.

'But, Ali,' said Owen, astounded, 'I could have all the women in the quarter for that sum!'

'That, too, later,' said Ali.

'Let us now turn to the boll weevil,' said the speaker on the platform.

Owen looked along the row of chairs for a means of escape. All the seats were taken, however, and to extricate himself would cause such a disruption that he thought better and resigned himself to the rest of the lecture.

'The rise of Egypt from bankruptcy to prosperity,' declared the speaker, 'can fairly be attributed to two causes: Cromer and cotton!'

'Hear, hear!'

'Modern irrigation, investment from overseas and the freeing of the fellahin, these were the things which provided a sound basis for the expansion of cotton production—'

'The freeing of the fellahin?' interrupted an incredulous voice from the back.

The speaker put down his notes.

'Yes, sir, the freeing of the fellahin. By giving fellahin the right to possess their own land, Lord Cromer transformed them from poverty-stricken serfs owing allegiance to feudal Turkish pashas to—'

'Poverty-stricken peasants owing everything to the bank! That's not freedom!'

There were cries of protest.

'Mr Chairman,' someone called out, 'isn't this a political point?'

'Yes, it is,' said the Chairman. 'This is not a political

meeting, Mr Sidki. May I ask you, please, to keep your remarks in order?'

'Thank you, Mr Chairman,' said the lecturer, mopping his brow—it was extremely hot in the large tent—'I was certainly under the impression, when I agreed to address the Khedivial Agricultural Society, that I was being asked for a scientific contribution. I'm not in the business of making political speeches.'

'Quite so.'

'I just want to say this: Egypt wouldn't be where it is today if it didn't have the wealth, experience and expertise of England behind it!'

'Hear, hear!'

'But that *is* a political speech!' cried the persistent voice from the back.

The Chairman decided it was time to move the meeting on.

'If I were you, Mr Hiscock, I would stick to cotton,' he advised.

'Yes, well, it's all connected. My point is that everything in Egypt depends on cotton. The economy is based on the success of the cotton crop. And now it's all being threatened by the boll weevil.'

The speaker, more at home with figures than words, produced statistics to show the crop loss resulting from the weevil's depredations.

'Could you put a value on that, Mr Hiscock?' asked the Chairman.

'£3.29 millions for the year just ended, at last year's prices.'

'Three million!'

Someone whistled.

'That's a lot! Think of the difference it would make to the country's finances at the present time!'

'There is no doubt,' said the speaker, 'that the shortfall

over the past three years has contributed materially to the present recession.'

'Is there anything that can be done about it?' someone asked.

The speaker glowed. There certainly was. But first he would have to explain the life cycle of the boll weevil.

Owen looked along the row again but the situation had not changed. If anything, the tent had become more crowded. When he had decided to go to the public meeting he had not expected that there would be such a large audience. The Khedivial Agricultural Society was clearly a thriving body.

The cycle began, the speaker explained, when the moth laid its eggs on the shoots of the young cotton plant in spring. When the eggs hatched out, the worms burrowed into the plant and fed upon it. The worm then came out again and formed a chrysalis from which it emerged later as the boll-worm moth.

'For our purposes, though,' said the speaker, 'the crucial thing is the timing.'

The gradual increase in temperature during the summer meant that most eggs hatched out in September, just when the cotton crop was becoming ready for picking. The first picking, early in the month, was not greatly affected; the second, later, showed significant depredation; and the third, in a bad year, could be a total loss.

'If, therefore,' said the speaker, 'we could bring the ripening of the crop forward, were it only by a couple of weeks, we would increase the yield significantly.'

'And how might this be done?'

'By changing the seed,' said Mr Hiscock triumphantly.

There was a rustle of interest around the tent.

'I can report that the Society has developed a new strain of seed which allows the crop to mature earlier.'

The audience burst into applause. The Chairman

allowed it to continue for some minutes and then rapped his gavel.

'But this is very important!' said a man, standing up, at the front. 'Lancashire depends on Egypt for its cotton.'

'It's pretty important to the fellahin, too,' said the irrepressible voice from the back.

'And the Society owns the rights in this?' asked the man at the front.

'Yes.'

'Excellent! Excellent!'

He sat down but then at once jumped up again.

'How soon can we have sufficient stocks to start selling?'

'Virtually immediately. Although, of course, it will take a year or two to build up stocks to the level at which we can replace all other seeds.'

'Excellent!'

'Excuse me,' said a new, diffident voice. 'Has the seed been properly field-tested?'

'Ah, Mr Aziz,' said the Chairman, with a certain lack of warmth. 'From the Department of Agriculture.'

'Of course it's been properly tested!' said the lecturer indignantly.

'I ask only because I saw the results of the last trials and they showed that the seed had a tendency to deteriorate on re-sowing.'

'Those were the first trials. We have, of course, improved the strain since.'

'And there is no deterioration? It's important, you see,' said Mr Aziz, shy but sticking to his guns, 'because the fellahin always keep back some seed to sow the following year.'

'They can always come back to us for new ones. In fact, that might be an advantage.'

'One moment, Mr Chairman!' called the persistent Mr Sidki from the back. 'Is Mr Aziz saying that the fellahin could be tricked into buying seed which it is known has a tendency to deteriorate?'

There were shouts of protest.

'Mr Aziz is saying nothing of the sort,' said the Chairman coldly. 'He was merely asking a question.'

'It's not the question that I'm bothered about; it's the answer.'

'Mr Sidki, really! The Society, I can assure you, is as committed to the interests of the fellahin as you are yourself!'

'It just sounded as if they were the ones who were being asked to bear the costs if things went wrong.'

'They're the ones who stand to gain most!' someone called out.

'I don't know about that,' said Mr Sidki. 'I think the ones who stand to gain most are the ones who sell them the seed and lend them the money with which to buy it!'

It was some time, amid the uproar, before the Chairman could be heard banging his gavel.

'I think,' he said, 'that this would be a good point at which to close the meeting.'

Afterwards, they all moved out on to the lawn for a cup of tea. The meeting was taking place, by kind permission of the Consul-General, in the grounds of what Old India hands—and there were lots of Old India hands—persisted in calling the Residency.

Small groups gathered among the rose-beds. Their behaviour was different, however, from that of the groups which annually gathered on the Consul-General's lawn; they actually looked at the roses.

By no means all the audience was English. There was a considerable sprinkling of sober-suited, be-tarbooshed Egyptian effendi. Owen wondered who they were. Employees of the society? Managers who worked for the big pashas who still owned over two-thirds of Egypt's cultivable land?

He recognized Aziz, the one who came from the Department of Agriculture. He was standing on his own and appeared to be rather out of it.

Owen went across to him.

'I was interested in the point you made,' he said. 'Do you think there's a real risk of the seed deteriorating?'

'Hard to say. The Society usually knows what it's doing. But that's what usually happens when you try to produce a new strain of seed. You think you've made a permanent alteration but after a generation or two it regresses.'

'You're a scientist yourself?'

'An entomologist.'

'Just the man for the Department of Agriculture.'

'Well . . .' Mr Aziz looked doubtful. 'I tried to get a job with the Society but of course there's a lot of competition.'

'Less so for the Ministry?'

'The Society is very well established.'

'Too well established,' a brisk voice joined in. It was the pushful Mr Sidki. He was a short, burly man, dressed in an extremely expensive dark suit and full of energy. He shook hands warmly

'The Mamur Zapt,' he said. 'So at last you've got round to it. Well, better late than never. Nice to see you here.'

He turned to Mr Aziz and took him confidingly by the arm.

'A good point you made just now! Excellent! I can see you're a man to watch.' He took a card out of his pocket and gave it to Mr Aziz. 'Sidki. Abdul Sidki.'

Mr Aziz looked at the card and his eyes rounded. 'Mr Sidki—!'

Sidki patted him on the arm. 'We must have a word some time. Come and see me at the Assembly. Before too long. We're always on the lookout for bright young men.'

Owen remembered now who he was. He was a Member

of the Legislative Assembly, one of the radicals; he did not actually belong to the new Nationalist Party—he had his own political ambitions—but was one of its most prominent sympathizers in the House.

'Thank you, Mr Sidki—'

Sidki patted him again. 'But now, if you'll excuse me, I'd like a word with the Mamur Zapt. That, too, is overdue.'

Aziz withdrew, impressed. Sidki now took Owen confidentially by the arm.

'Good to see you here, my dear fellow. So at last they're beginning to listen! Pretty goings on, don't you think? Not content with making a fortune out of selling fertilizer, they now want to get everyone to change to a new seed. And at a higher price, I'll be bound!'

'It seemed to have advantages.'

Mr Sidki waved these aside.

'And disadvantages, too, if that young man is right. And it's the fellahin who'll pick those up. But, Captain, Owen—' he clutched him more firmly—'advantages or disadvantages, that's not the point. The point is that the benefit will all be going to private interests.'

'The Khedivial Agricultural Society hardly counts as private—'

Mr Sidki withdrew his arm, turned and stared at Owen.

'But surely, Captain Owen, you know? The Khedivial Society is big business. It is not like, what shall I say, the local Agricultural Society in, say, Maidenhead. (And, incidentally, Captain Owen, I do find some English place-names distastefully explicit.) The Khedivial Agricultural Society is one of the most powerful businesses in Egypt.'

'Oh, come—'

'Think for a moment!' Mr Sidki insisted. 'It already supplies nearly half the country's new seed. And this in a country where the cultivation of seed is the chief livelihood. You don't do that on one pound members' subscriptions, Captain Owen!'

'Perhaps not, but—'

Mr Sidki seized Owen again and brought his mouth dramatically close to Owen's ear.

'Where does the money come from?' he hissed. 'And where does it go? There are no published accounts. We've asked for them but been refused. It's not a public body, you see. The whole thing needs looking at.'

He stepped back a little and waved at someone over Owen's shoulder with the ready, practised smile of the politician.

'Especially now,' he said, 'when we're being asked to make such large sums available to the Agricultural Bank.'

'I'm afraid I don't see the connection.'

Mr Sidki looked at Owen as if he could not believe anyone could be so innocent. Then he shrugged his shoulders slightly as if to say that if that was what Owen wanted, then he was prepared to go on with the game.

'It's a cosy little arrangement, isn't it? The Bank lends money to the fellahin so that they can buy seed. But it makes one condition: the seed has to be of good quality.'

He stopped meaningly.

'Well?'

'And who decides whether it is of good quality?'

'The Khedivial Agricultural Society?'

'Exactly. And, strangely enough, it only finds really satisfactory the seed which the Society itself has produced.' He smiled triumphantly and watched Owen closely. 'Cosy, isn't it?'

'And not accidental, you're suggesting?'

'I'm suggesting the arrangement needs examination to see if it's in the public interest.'

'Public audit?' murmured Owen, who had been learning fast recently.

Mr Sidki made a gesture of dismissal.

'Accountants look for consistencies; they don't look at

realities. Provided the story is consistent, they're not bothered whether it's true.'

'Hum, yes.'

'Otherwise, why would they let obviously dubious firms get away with it? Have you, Captain Owen, since you have been in Egypt, ever known auditors publicly qualify a firm's accounts?'

'No,' said Owen, who had only just heard there were auditors, 'er, no.'

'Exactly!' said Mr Sidki. 'So—?' He looked at Owen expectantly.

'You may be right, Mr Sidki, and this matter may need investigation. But I am not sure I am the one who should be conducting it.'

'A Parliamentary matter, you mean? Well, of course, you're quite right. A Select Commission—the obvious answer, I've proposed it myself. But the Government won't hear of it. And you can guess why! Vested interests, Captain Owen, vested interests! No, given the Government's attitude, I'm afraid, it's going to have to be someone completely independent.'

'The Parquet, perhaps—'

'The Parquet? Independent? A Government tool.'

'Nevertheless, Mr Sidki, I think you've been implying that there could be an issue of criminal law here. It's the Parquet that would have to handle that.'

'The case would never be called.'

'You see. I'm concerned only with political matters—'

'This *is* a political matter,' Mr Sidki declared.

He looked at Owen closely.

'You begin to worry me, Captain Owen. Can it be that you have received instructions . . . ?'

'Certainly not!'

'I am glad to hear it. If it is true. It would, of course, be something we would have to take up in the House. I hope it needn't come to that.'

Owen shrugged. 'You must act as you think fit, Mr Sidki.'

'You see, it is becoming a matter of some urgency. That agreement or arrangement or whatever it is—that understanding which no one outside the Bank understands—with the Department of Agriculture—'

'You are well informed.'

'Yes. We are.'

Unexpectedly, Mr Sidki hesitated.

'Or were. Until recently.'

'How recently, Mr Sidki?'

Mr Sidki's eyes met his.

'Until Osman Fingari was killed.'

CHAPTER 6

'Killed, Captain Owen?'

Mr Fehmi was shocked.

'Surely not! I thought we had agreed that this was to be a case of suicide.'

'We didn't agree it was "to be" anything. We thought it *was* a case of suicide.'

'Well, yes, of course. That's what I meant.'

The Parquet lawyer looked at Owen with injured brown eyes.

'How could it be anything else? He took prussic acid. No shadow of doubt! The post-mortem—your own colleague, Captain Owen—'

'Yes, yes. I've no doubt about that.'

'Then wherein lies your doubt? We found the bottle beside him in the wastepaper basket. A small brown bottle,' said Mr Fehmi in injured tones, 'which he had bought the day before. Bought it himself, Captain Owen. We found the shop. Descriptions fit. Why all this complication?'

'I am merely reporting an accusation.'

'From whom, Captain Owen? From whom?'

Mr Fehmi's shoulders bowed, as if they had suddenly been called on to support the weight of the whole guilty world in addition to the weight of Cairo's guilty world, the burden which they already carried.

'I am not at liberty to say.'

Mr Fehmi sat back. 'An anonymous informant? Did he produce any evidence in support of his claim?'

'Well, no—'

Mr Fehmi shook his head pityingly. 'Captain Owen!'

Owen felt called on to justify himself.

'The charge came from someone whom neither you nor I can afford to disregard.'

'Ah well, in that case—' said Mr Fehmi. 'That's different. That's quite different. But I still—I don't see how it *could* be anything other than suicide, Captain Owen. He was in a disturbed state of mind—I haven't gone into that side, you requested me not to, but I've heard sufficient—'

'He was certainly in a disturbed state of mind.'

'He bought the bottle, he took it to his office, he almost certainly drank it *in* his office. He didn't drink it before and he didn't go out of his office. That's where he was found, with the bottle beside him—'

Mr Fehmi shrugged his shoulders in bewilderment that any could question.

'Did anyone go in?'

'No.'

'You've checked?'

'I've checked.'

'Coffee? Did he have coffee?'

'Yes. I used that to establish time of death.'

'Presumably Abdul Latif took it in to him?'

'The orderly? Yes. But, Captain Owen, what are you suggesting? That the orderly poisoned him? Administered it with the coffee, perhaps? The taste so frightful that he couldn't tell the difference?'

Fearing that he had gone too far, Mr Fehmi patted Owen apologetically on the knee. 'A jest,' he said, 'a jest!'

'Thank you.'

'Killed?' He shook his head slowly but firmly. 'No, Captain Owen, I think not.'

He rose from his chair.

'I suggest you go back to your informant and tell him that he is mistaken.'

He reached out his hand in farewell.

'There is not a shred of evidence to connect this sad event with anyone other than Mr Fingari himself.'

'Not now that you have removed his diary,' said Owen.

Mr Fehmi fell back into his seat.

'Removed his diary? Captain Owen! What are you saying? What are you saying, please? I reject this imputation. I— I—'

'Do you deny that the diary is in your possession?'

'Deny it? Of course I deny it!'

'I would not answer so quickly, Mr Fehmi. As the investigating official, you have every right to remove a piece of evidence. What you do not have is the power to withhold it.'

Mr Fehmi licked his lips.

'I—I deny absolutely— Really, Captain Owen, this is outrageous!'

'I would like to see it, please.'

'I have not got it!'

'It is no longer in your possession?'

'It never was in my possession!'

'You took it from Fingari's desk.'

'This is—this is quite unacceptable—'

'I hope not. What would be unacceptable would be for you to keep it from me.'

'I object most strongly, Captain Owen—'

'Unacceptable,' said Owen with emphasis. 'By which I mean that my Administration would not be prepared to accept it.'

Mr Fehmi licked his lips again. Owen could see that he was weighing the rival strengths of the Minister-backed Parquet and the British Administration-backed Mamur Zapt. But this was precisely the sort of political calculation that Mr Fehmi was not good at. He hung there uncertainly.

Owen decided to make it easier for him.

'I am not suggesting that you part with the diary. What I had in mind was merely that as colleagues working together we sit down here and share our impressions of the case, with the diary, and other evidence, naturally in front of us.'

'That—that would be more acceptable,' said Mr Fehmi.

He still appeared, however, to be in difficulty.

'It would be in confidence, of course,' said Owen. 'There is no reason why anyone other than the two of us should ever know that our—our conversation had taken place.'

Some, at least, of Mr Fehmi's difficulties were disappearing.

'And each of us, of course, will have our areas of reticence, where we would prefer the other not to press us.'

Mr Fehmi visibly relaxed.

'I think I could cooperate on that basis,' he said.

'Good.'

'But—but there's still a difficulty. I would have to borrow the book back.'

'Borrow it back? Who has it, then?'

Mr Fehmi hesitated.

'Come, Mr Fehmi, there has to be some basis of trust between us.'

Mr Fehmi still hesitated.

'Cannot you at least tell me at the general level?'

Mr Fehmi took the plunge.

'It is with the Minister,' he said.

'Minister? Which Minister? Parquet or Agriculture?'

Mr Fehmi hung his head.

'That—that is an area of reticence,' he said.

'Yes, it's beautiful, darling,' said Owen.

'You don't sound very enthusiastic,' said Zeinab. 'Don't you like it?'

'Oh yes, oh yes. It's—it's just the price.'

'If you want good things you have to pay for them,' said Zeinab. 'Anyway, I'm the one who's paying, not you.'

'Yes, but if—when we get married—'

'You can pay,' said Zeinab generously.

'That's just it. I'm not sure that I'll be able to. My salary, you know—'

'Get a higher one.'

'That's easier said than done.'

'Oh, I don't know. You're a clever chap, everybody knows that. *I* think you're brilliant—usually, that is. You don't value yourself as you should, that's the problem. Why don't you just ask them?'

'It doesn't work in that way. Anyway, I'd have to be promoted to Field Marshal before we could afford hats like that.'

'Oh dear!' said Zeinab.

'Look, does it matter that much? If we love each other, I mean?'

'Money certainly does matter,' said Zeinab.

If the formal gardens in which the Ministries were set owed something in design to France, the techniques their gardeners employed were traditionally Egyptian. An intricate system of irrigation channels connected the gardens to a water-wheel on the river bank which every so often scooped up water from the river and fed it through the gardens.

This had recently been supplemented by modern pipelines and stopcocks but the approach remained essentially the same: to water by flooding rather than by sprinkling.

Every Thursday the men from the Water Board came round and opened the stopcocks and flooded the gardens, including the lawns, to a depth of two or three inches. The waters soon subsided, leaving both ground and, more to the point in their view, gardeners fresh.

The event soon became part of the regular entertainment of the city. Mothers brought their children to play, men brought their donkeys to drink and birds in their hundreds flocked down to paddle and bathe and generally take the waters. Owen this morning counted bulbuls and sparrows and weavers and warblers, bee-eaters and hoopoes and the usual vulgar crowd of palm-doves.

A little group of men was gathered around some sickly-looking shrubs in a corner of the garden and as Owen went past there was much shaking of heads going on.

'I don't understand it,' someone was saying. He looked up and saw Owen. 'Oh, hallo, old boy.'

It was the Chairman of the Agricultural Society. He straightened up and dusted his hands.

'We'll just have to try it, I suppose,' he said.

He walked along the path to join Owen.

'Problems?' asked Owen.

The Chairman grimaced. 'The Khedive got these plants in especially from Nepal. We didn't think they'd take. But he expects us to do something about it.'

'Fertilizer?' said Owen, banging his head against the horizon of his horticultural knowledge.

'The whole environment's not right. Of course, what we could do is take them out and put them under glass and create an artificial environment, but . . .'

He shrugged and dismissed the topic.

'Glad to see you at our meeting the other day. A breakthrough, you know, a real breakthrough.'

'The new seed certainly does seem to have advantages.'

'It could make all the difference.'

'That chap from the Ministry had doubts, though.'

'They always have doubts. Listen to them and nothing would ever get done. Until we came along nothing ever *was* done. Do you know the story of the Society?'

'No.'

'Well, it was set up by the Khedive. The old boy's interested in horticulture—he's always getting things like those shrubs—and he reckoned that what was needed was some body which would encourage research and spread knowledge. Well, he talked and talked, but no one would listen to him and in the end he decided to set one up himself.'

'Good for him!'

'Just what I say! You know, I've got a lot of time for the old boy. Others haven't, I know, but I speak as I find. And I've always found him very positive. Full of ideas, you know.'

'Really?'

'Yes. Not just on horticulture. Roads, development, that sort of thing.'

'Really?'

'Yes. A real force for modernization. Surprising, that, isn't it? A hereditary ruler and all that. But he's on our side, you know. A real modernizer.'

'In some things, yes.'

'Politics? Ah well, we'd better not go into that. Anyway, he set up the Society and from that moment we've never looked back. Retains an interest in it, you know. Prince Hafiz is on the Board. Did you know that? A great asset.'

'I'm sure. But, tell me, where does the Society get its money from? It has such a range of interests, does so many things—'

'I know. Terrific, isn't it? Sometimes I'm surprised myself. Well, it makes it.'

'Makes it?'

'Yes. The old boy said, when he set it up, that he didn't

want to keep pouring money in. After the first lot, that was it. So we had to jolly well make it. And we have!'

'But surely there is a constant need for capital—'

'Oh, various people have chipped in. The Cotton-Growers' Association, some of the big firms, the banks—'

'You don't publish any accounts, I understand?'

'Why should we? It's our business, old boy. Private matter entirely.'

'It's just that the scale—'

'What's wrong with that? Tribute to our success, old boy. Got the whole country moving.'

'It makes people ask questions.'

The Chairman stopped and turned towards Owen.

'Who? Who's asking questions?'

'The politicians.'

The Chairman dismissed them with a gesture.

'Rabble-rousers. Ask a lot of questions, don't ever actually *do* anything. They're riding on our backs, you know. We're carrying them—and they're making us pay for the pleasure! Rich, isn't it?'

'If they're asking questions, why not give them some answers?'

'I say, old boy, that's a bit radical!' There was a little pause. 'What are they asking questions about?'

'The tie-up between the Society and the Agricultural Bank for a start.'

'One of the most imaginative things the Government's ever done. You heard Hiscock the other day? Free the fellahin and then lend them the money to farm for themselves. It's transformed agriculture, believe me!'

'I gather there's a question about the conditions on which the money is lent.'

'The rate of interest? Don't know much about it. But I'll tell you this: however high it is, it's nothing like as high as that charged by the money-lenders they've been going to up to now!'

'Not just the interest: the seed's got to be approved, I gather.'

'Quite right, too. The seed they were using ... No wonder the yield was so low!'

'The Society vets the seed, I gather.'

'Yes, that's one of our services.'

'And favours its own.'

'It's the best. You should see the reports from our labs.'

'That carries risks, though.'

'Risks? What sort of risks?'

'Political risks.'

'Those damned politicians again?'

Barclay went past as Owen sat waiting for Paul.

'Can I catch you a moment?'

'Of course.'

Barclay slid into the seat opposite.

'It's about that road. You got me worried the other day, you know, when you said someone might be buying ahead in the Derb Aiah area. That's a *long* way ahead. It's sort of second phase. They'd have to be pretty sure the first phase, the north–south road, was going to go ahead. Well . . .'

'Yes?'

'There's an application in to the Ministry to be allowed to proceed with the development.'

'The north–south road? Going down the east side? Through the Old City?'

Barclay nodded. 'That's right,' he said, his eyes solemn behind his little round, gold-framed glasses.

'But I thought it wasn't ever going to happen?'

'It keeps coming up. It's just that we never give permission and that there's never any money. That's the important point, really. Nobody gives a damn whether we give permission or not.'

'Well, there certainly isn't likely to be any money this time.'

'No-o.' But Barclay sounded doubtful.

'Is there?'

'We've had to make provision for it this year in our budget.'

'I thought you never gave permission?'

'We don't. We won't,' Barclay assured him.

'Then why is it in the budget?'

'The Minister said it had to be. It will be struck out later, of course. All the same . . .'

'I don't like it. Once these things get on paper, they never get off it.'

Barclay stood up.

'Just thought you'd like to know,' he said.

Paul pooh-poohed the idea.

'Not a hope! I can tell you the attitude to the budget this year: chop anything that moves, even if it only wriggles. A project of this size? Ha ha!'

'I don't like it. Once it's in the budget—'

'That doesn't mean to say it will ever happen. There are a lot of things we include in the budget just so that we can cut them out. They always want saving, so it's as well to have something you can offer.'

'It's a dangerous game, though, Paul. Suppose they nodded it through?'

'In a fit of absence of mind, you mean, like we acquired the colonies? There'll be no absence of mind this time, not in this year's budget round, I can assure you!'

'Yes but, taken together with this application for planning permission—'

'I don't know what that's about,' Paul confessed. 'Perhaps the Khedive's behind it and they're telling him to put it in just to keep his mind off important things.'

'But this *is* important!'

'He has enthusiasms, you see. We let him indulge them so long as they don't actually ever get anywhere.'

Owen was not convinced. However, at that moment an orderly came rushing into the room and called Paul to the telephone.

Paul was upset.

'Things are reaching a pretty pass,' he said darkly, 'when economic crises start interfering with a chap's drinking.'

Ali was waiting for him as he came down the steps of his office.

'Effendi, you're in luck!' he greeted him. 'She will see you this afternoon.'

'Good.'

'She pines for you, she pants for you. Her breast burns for you.'

'She didn't say that!'

'Well, not quite that,' Ali admitted. 'But that's what she means.'

'She doesn't mean anything of the sort. Now, what is it?'

'Strike while the iron is hot, effendi,' Ali advised, 'and then sweet success will be the fruit of your labours.'

'Thank you. And now let's get down to what she actually said.'

'Be at the El Amr mosque just before evening prayers. She will be there with her cousin. Her cousin knows all and will assist.'

He pocketed the milliemes.

'I myself,' he said airily, 'will, of course, be there.'

The El Amr mosque, perhaps the oldest in Cairo, was no longer in regular use. Palm trees grew in its central courtyard. The side colonnades had fallen. Only the marble columns of the central *liwan* remained.

Yet use of some sort there still was. Here and there among the pillars the black forms of women could be seen. The aura lingered in a place which had once held power and women came for their own purposes.

They came to certain spots especially. One of these was a carved recess in a wall which looked like an antique altar. Its two little columns had worn away leaving holes the size of cuttle-fish. These were where for generations mothers had rubbed the stone with lemon so that their babies might cry when their mouths were held against it; for if they went away from Amr's Mosque without a cry, was not this a sign that they would grow to be dumb?

As Owen watched, two women, both heavily veiled and in the shapeless black which rendered unprovocative any suggestion of woman's form, one of them carrying a baby, came through the pillars and went up to the altar.

The baby, lifted from its warm cocoon in the woman's arms, gave a little cry as it was held to the stonework. Satisfied, though hardly surprised, the woman folded it back again and then sat down on a fallen pillar nearby and gave it suck.

The other woman moved off into the pillars. Owen moved after her.

'Aisha.'

'Effendi.'

'I have something to ask you.'

She moved to where a pillar stood close against a wall. Between the wall and the pillar there was just space for a person to stand. She pushed Owen into it so that he could not be seen and then stood with her back against the pillar as if resting or in thought.

'Ask on.'

'There is a man, a friend of your brother's. His name is Jabir. Can you tell me anything about him?'

Aisha did not reply. He thought that perhaps she had not heard him, and repeated the question.

Aisha made a little gesture with her hand.

'I know him,' she whispered.

'He was at school with Osman. Or perhaps at college.'

'School. They were always together. Osman always wanted to be with him. He seemed fascinated by him. But he was a bad boy, effendi. He was always getting Osman to do things he shouldn't.'

'Like what?'

'Little things. Silly things. Playing jokes on other boys, on the teachers. And it was always Osman who got caught. I said to him: "Why are you so silly? Why do you do what he tells you? He will get you into trouble." But he wouldn't listen to me, effendi. He—' She stopped.

'Yes?'

'He went with him all the more. As if he could not stop. It used to hurt me, especially when I learned they were doing nasty things together—'

'What things, Aisha?'

Aisha swallowed.

'There was a bird,' she said. 'It had hurt its wing and could not fly. Jabir took it and—and tormented it, effendi. He made Osman . . . And Osman did it, that is what I could not understand. I asked him how he could do a thing like that? I said, "Jabir is making you evil." And then—' She stopped.

'Yes?'

'Osman must have told him what I had said. For after that . . .'

'Yes?'

'Jabir turned his attention to me. He began to say nasty things about me, dirty things. And then one day he told Osman he wouldn't speak to him any more unless he arranged a meeting.'

'A meeting? With you?'

'Yes. Osman asked me. I refused, of course. I was angry. I told him not to be stupid, that he was being made a fool of. But . . . but . . .' Her voice faltered.

'Yes?'

'Osman was so unhappy. Jabir was always teasing him, out loud, to all the other boys. "He is tied to his sister's skirts," he said. "He does whatever she tells him." It went on and on and Osman was so unhappy—he didn't want to go to school—that in the end, well . . .'

'You saw him?'

'Yes. He—he was disgusting. He said things . . . I wouldn't see him again. Not even for Osman . . . In fact, though, he didn't ask again. That, it seemed, was enough. All he wanted. Just to talk—talk like that . . .' Her voice trailed away.

This was not quite what Owen had expected to hear.

'I am sorry,' he said awkwardly.

'I don't know what he did to Osman afterwards.' Her voice was almost inaudible. 'One day Osman didn't come home. They brought him to us later. He had tried to throw himself in front of a train. I think it frightened even Jabir for after that things were better. They stayed away from each other for the rest of the time they were at school. But then . . .'

She gestured her bewilderment.

'They started seeing each other again. It was after Osman had started working at the Ministry. I could not believe it. "What?" I said. "After what he had done?" "All that is past," said Osman. Soon they were friends as before. One day he brought him home. Afterwards, when Jabir left, he said: "Greet your sister for me, Osman." I said: "I do not want greetings from such as he."

'Osman said nothing. But the next day he took me aside and said: "You must not talk like that. All that is in the past. Encourage him. He is interested in you."

'"I am not interested in him," I said. Osman shrugged. "You are getting old," he said, "and time is going by. Beggars cannot be choosers."'

Aisha looked at Owen.

'That was two years ago,' she said. 'Now I am even older.'

'A man looks for all sorts of things in a wife,' Owen said.

Aisha shrugged.

'Perhaps. "I would rather grow old alone," I said, "than be wife to a man like that." "What do you have against him?" Osman asked. "What do you see in him?" I countered, for I was angry that he should have forgotten. "He knows how to rise,"' said Osman.

Aisha's cousin appeared through the pillars.

'"And you think he will show you how to rise?" I said to Osman. "He has friends who have helped him and could help me." "If?" I asked.'

'What did he reply?'

'He walked away. But I think, effendi,' she said, looking him in the face, 'that if there was a beginning, then that could have been it.'

The cousin began to signal imperatively.

'I shall have to go, effendi.'

As she walked away, Ali suddenly appeared beside him, studying the women in apparent bewilderment.

'Haven't we got this wrong, effendi,' he asked. 'Oughtn't the babies to be coming later?'

CHAPTER 7

'There's trouble in the Derb Aiah district,' said Nikos.

Owen reached for his sun helmet. He kept both sun helmet and tarboosh in his office but when missiles started flying sun helmet was best.

'What sort of trouble?'

'Riot. The police are down there.'

Owen hurried along the corridor. As he went past the office of the Deputy Commandant he looked in but McPhee was not there. He went on and into the orderly room.

'Where's the Bimbashi?'

'At Kasr el Aini, effendi.'

Kasr el Aini was on the other side of town.

'There's a riot in the Derb Aiah.'

'Yes, effendi.'

'I'm going over. Tell the Bimbashi when he gets back.'

Strictly speaking, immediate policing was the preserve of the police. The Mamur Zapt, however, was responsible for the preservation of order in the city and Owen took the view that the first thing was to get on top of any disorder and argue about the division of responsibility afterwards.

There was a one-horse arabeah in the street outside the Bab el Khalk; one-horse, unfortunately, in every sense. Owen jumped in and told the driver to hurry to the Derb Aiah.

This was asking for the impossible. The cab proceeded at its usual slow amble along the Khalig el Masri, past the House of the Grand Mufti, past the Syrian Church, the Maronite Church, the Armenian Church, the Coptic Church, the Greek Orthodox Church and the French Church and, some time later, at last, turned into the Derb Aiah.

Where there was no sign of a riot. The street was deserted.

Suspiciously deserted. Shops were closed, stalls abandoned. There was just one solitary figure, an old man limping along with a stick.

Owen caught up with him.

'Where is it?' he said.

The man lifted his stick and pointed down a side-street. Owen hurried ahead. He found himself in a warren of mediæval alleyways and streets. All were deserted.

He stopped and listened.

This was puzzling. Usually you could hear. There was, indeed, a low murmuring, but . . .

He plunged on. At the end of a street he saw people.

He came up behind them. Tall, he was able to see over their heads. There was a little square, not so much a square as a widening of the street where several alleyways joined. The space was crammed with people.

But they were all quiet! What sort of riot was this?

He began to push his way through the crowd. Everyone was looking in one direction, towards the other side of the square.

All he could see was an old fountain-house. There was the fountain chamber, at ground level and open to the street, and there above it the usual arched second chamber.

There was someone standing in one of the arches. It was a woman, short and stout and dressed in black. Her arms were folded.

There seemed something familiar about her.

Owen pushed closer and looked up: the Widow Shawquat!

Around the bottom of the fountain-house was a thin line of harassed-looking policemen.

'What's going on?' said Owen, in Arabic.

'By God, she is putting salt on their tails!' said someone in front of him with relish.

The voice, too, seemed familiar. Its owner looked round. It was Owen's friend, the barber.

'What's up there?'

'The *kuttub*.'

The school. The Widow Shawquat's school. It all began to fall into place.

'The police came, did they?'

'Yes. Her son was hearing the children say their lessons and the police came and said "The *kuttub* belongs to someone else now: out you go!" And Abdul said: "I will send for my mother!" And the police said. "Ho ho!" And then the Widow Shawquat came.'

'What happened?'

'She kicked their ass.'

One of the constables at the foot of the fountain-house, hearing the exchange, turned round.

'She attacked me brutally, effendi!' he said indignantly. 'She smote me savagely in the side!'

'She kicked you up the ass!' said the barber.

'She thrust me from the *kuttub*!'

'You, a policeman! What sort of man is this? To allow a woman to put him out!'

'I'd like to see you try!' retorted the constable. 'You wouldn't do any better!'

'Twenty policemen? One woman?' scoffed somebody from the crowd.

'There weren't twenty! There were just three of us,' protested the constable who had been assaulted.

'And then you called for reinforcements!' jeered the scoffer in the crowd. 'One woman!'

'One woman!' said the barber indignantly. He jumped up on to the steps of the fountain-house and turned to address the crowd. 'One woman! Savagely assaulted!'

'Here, wait a minute,' said the policeman. 'You've got it wrong. We were the ones who were savagely assaulted.'

'A woman of the people!' cried the barber. 'One of us!'

'Yes, yes!'

The crowd, excited, began to stir.

'Brutally attacked!' cried the barber.

'Shame! Shame!'

'Her first, us next!'

'It certainly will be you if you don't shut up,' warned one of the policemen.

'They are picking on our women!'

The policemen began to look anxious.

'What are we going to do?' one of them called to Owen over the heads of the crowd.

'Who's in charge here?'

The constables pushed forward a reluctant corporal.

'What shall I do, effendi? I ought to arrest her for disturbing the peace, but . . .'

'Just try it! Just try it!' cried the barber.

'Shall I knock him on the head?' asked one of the constables.

'You ought to go up and reason with her, Hamid,' said
one of the constables urgently.

The corporal seemed unwilling.

'Yes!' said the constable enthusiastically. 'Go up and talk
to her sweetly, Hamid!'

'She might kick *my* ass,' objected the corporal. 'That
would be bad for discipline.'

'Call yourself a man?' cried the barber.

The corporal turned on him threateningly. The Widow
Shawquat was one thing; an ordinary street agitator quite
another.

'Are you disturbing the peace?'

The barber skipped hastily back into the crowd. With
two or three rows in between him and the constables he
felt bolder.

'I'm not: she is,' he said. 'Why don't you do something
about her?'

'Yes, why not!' taunted the crowd.

'We could rush her,' said one of the constables
doubtfully.

'Right!' said the corporal. 'You go first.'

The constables looked at the staircase uncertainly.

'You rush her,' shouted someone in the crowd—it may
have been the barber—'and we'll rush you!'

The crowd, good-humoured up to now and enjoying
watching the police's dilemma, suddenly surged menac-
ingly forward.

The constables paled and fell back.

The crowd pushed forward again, driving them back and
back until they came to the front of the stairs. One or two
of the constables were forced up it. As more and more came

on to the stairs, the ones at the top, realizing who awaited them above, clung to the balustrade in an attempt to resist their upward progression.

Owen had been trying to force his way through but the people in front of him were so tightly jammed together that he had been unable to move. The sudden eddies of the crowd, however, gave him some leverage and he succeeded in breaking through to where the policemen huddled on the stairs.

'Back!' he shouted. 'Back! Make room! I will talk to the Widow Shawquat!'

'This I long to see,' said a satirical voice from the crowd.

'Who's he?'

'What's an Effendi doing here?'

'It is the Mamur Zapt!' said a well-known voice from above. 'My Deliverer has come!'

The Widow appeared at the top of the stairs.

'Make way, make way there!' she shouted. 'Get out of it! Let him come up! Praise be to God! The Mamur Zapt has heard the prayers of a poor defenceless woman.'

The crowd fell silent.

'By God, he has!' said someone in an amazed voice. 'That was quick!'

The police parted, only too willingly, to give Owen passage.

At the top of the stairs he found a class of children, goggle-eyed, the redoubtable Widow, and a slight, gentle-faced man shrinking back against the wall not so much in fear as in embarrassment, as if he was willing the walls to open and cover him. As Owen appeared, he buried his face in his hands.

The Widow Shawquat was less bashful.

'Protector of the Poor!' she hailed Owen joyfully. 'Saviour of the Shawquats!'

'What is all this?'

The Widow's moment had come, however. She seized

Owen by the hands and drew him forward to the balustrade which ran round the whole of the upper storey.

'Behold!' she cried to the crowd below. 'Our Defender has come! He will right our wrongs! He will cast down the Mighty from their Seats!'

The crowd, thrilled beyond measure, and believing that the millennium had come, began to cry out in ecstasy. On the outskirts, two dervishes began to whirl.

'What are the police to him?' scoffed the Widow.

Beyond the houses, from somewhere in the warren of streets, came a loud honking. Owen knew what it was. It was the police force's one car.

A moment later it appeared in one of the side-streets. Its roof was open and there, standing up beside the driver, was the tall, thin figure of the Deputy Commandant of the Cairo Police, McPhee. With him, in the back, were armed policemen.

'Disperse!' shouted McPhee. 'Disperse at once! Return to your homes!'

The car pressed forward into the crowd.

People, panic-stricken, began to fall out of its way. Those at the edge of the crowd started to run off up the side-streets.

The car came to a halt. The policemen jumped out of the car and fanned out, guns at the ready.

'Disperse!' shouted McPhee. 'At once.'

'It's all right,' shouted Owen.

McPhee looked up, bewildered.

'Owen! What are you doing here?'

What, indeed, thought Owen.

'And when I arrived,' said McPhee, 'there was Owen orchestrating the crowd!'

'Managing it,' said Owen. 'I was getting it to calm down.'

'It didn't look like that to me,' said McPhee.

'You should have been there a moment or two earlier!'

'I came as quickly as I could,' said McPhee, taking this as a reproach. 'The car was being cleaned.'

Garvin sighed. He was the Commandant of the Cairo Police, weary in the ways of Egyptian policing.

'As far as I can see, there was no actual violence.'

'Three constables have lodged a complaint,' said McPhee stiffly. 'Undue violence perpetrated against their persons.'

'She kicked them up the backside,' said Owen.

'That's what I meant, sir,' said McPhee, turning to Garvin. 'Whose side is he on?'

'If that was the extent of the violence,' said Garvin, 'I've seen worse cases: about twenty times a day.'

'It's the principle of the thing,' said McPhee severely.

Garvin sighed again.

'Is there any reason,' he asked, 'why we should give any time to this whatsoever?'

Owen hesitated. 'Yes, there is.'

He told them about the possible development of the Derb Aiah area. McPhee, especially, listened with interest.

'But that would take in the *tekke*,' he said.

'The little mosque with the blue tiles? All sparkle?'

'Yes.'

McPhee knew his mosques. He was an enthusiast less about things architectural than about things religious and collected shrines and feast-days and old Cairo saints with avidity. Garvin tolerated this eccentricity as he tolerated Owen's.

'It would be terrible if that was to go,' McPhee said.

'You think it could cause trouble?' Garvin asked Owen.

'I think there's something else that would cause more.'

He told them about the proposed north–south road.

'Through the City!' said McPhee, appalled.

'It'll never happen!' said Garvin dismissively.

'There's a planning application in.'

'Doesn't mean a thing.'

'The Khedive's keen.'

'Means even less.'

'I don't know about that. It could be another case like the Agricultural Society.'

'What?' said Garvin, caught off-balance and looking at Owen as if he had suddenly realized that he was suffering from sunstroke.

'When he couldn't get anywhere, he got on and did it himself.'

He told them about the founding of the Society.

Garvin looked at his watch.

'Yes, well, thank you. Can I suggest you follow up other things? Both of you.'

'Yussef,' said Owen severely, 'this is the second time in a month.'

'This is the first time, effendi. The other time was last month.'

'No, it wasn't. I've written it down in my little book. See?'

Yussef, the office orderly, could not read but could recognize the large letter which began his name; and also, alas, the figures alongside it.

'Effendi, I need it to buy seed.'

'That's what you told me last time. You said it was the planting season and that you needed the money to buy seed. What happened to it? What did you do with the money?'

'I used it to buy seed. Some of it. But I owed my brother some money, effendi. And also my sister. And then there was my uncle and aunt—'

'Look, I'm not supporting the whole family.'

He knew, however, that he was. Yussef, like many of the other orderlies, had left his native village and moved into the town in search of better paid employment. He still retained a strip of land in the village, however, which was now worked by his wife and children with occasional support from the rest of his family. The rest of the family were as much in debt as Yussef himself.

He regularly came to Owen for an advance on pay before the end of the month. Owen didn't mind that as he thought a month was a long time to wait for people as lowly-paid as the orderlies. He did feel, however, a certain responsibility for Yussef and tried to see that he didn't get too much into debt.

Unfortunately, the Government was not the only body to which Yussef owed money and there was not much Owen could do about the others. He lectured Yussef sternly and Yussef looked doleful but that was as far as it went.

'Two advances in a month! Yussef, if I gave you that, what would you have left? We would come to the end of the month and then there would be nothing. You would have to borrow again.'

'That's right, effendi,' said Yussef hopefully.

'Think of your children: what would they live on?'

'If you lend me the money, effendi, then with it I can buy hens and they will lay eggs. They can eat eggs.'

'I thought you wanted to spend it on seed?'

'Seed,' said Yussef vaguely, 'and hens.'

Owen gave up and agreed to advance Yussef a small sum. If they went on like this he would soon be paying him weekly.

That might be a good idea. He knew enough, however, about the state of Yussef's finances to realize that whatever he did would not go far towards solving Yussef's problem. The real problem was the huge backlog of debt that Yussef, like most fellahin, had accumulated over the years.

It was the responsibility of the paying off that sum from his earnings on the land that had driven Yussef to seek work in the City: that and the fact that work on the land was hard and he would much rather his wife did it than him.

A job in Government service was the great prize for

which everyone strove. The hours were short, the work, to
men accustomed to labouring long hours in the fields, easy;
the pay, though not high, was certain and regular. It was
a meal-ticket for life; and quite a lot of people lived on every
meal-ticket.

Yussef went off happily, while Owen thought about seed.

'You'd better speak to my father,' said Zeinab.

Nikos was on the phone when Owen entered his office. He
glanced up.

'The Parquet,' he said.

It was Mr Fehmi.

'About the, um, diary,' he said.

'Yes?'

'It's been, um, found.'

'Found?'

'Yes. In one of the filing cabinets. We must have missed
it.'

There was a little silence.

'I see,' said Owen.

Mr Fehmi met him with an apologetic smile.

'These things happen,' he said, shrugging his shoulders.

No pages had been cut out, as Owen had half expected,
nor, at cursory glance, were there any erasures. Crossings
out, though vigorous and complete, might have been Fingari's own. Nevertheless, Owen knew now that he would
not find the diary particularly helpful. All the same . . .

'I would like my people to work on it,' he said.

'Of course. I would like mine to, too,' said Fehmi. 'Here,
perhaps?'

The next time Owen looked in there were three men
working in the office: Georgiades, sitting at Osman Fingari's desk with the Appointments Diary open in front of
him; Mr Fehmi, beside him, peering over his shoulder: and

a third man, whom Owen did not know, one of Fehmi's presumably, taking notes.

'A working lunch,' said Mr Fehmi. 'The same people.'

Georgiades noted the date.

'The twenty-third,' said Mr Fehmi, clicking his fingers. The third man wrote it down.

'Any new names?' asked Owen.

'A few.'

He looked over Georgiades's shoulder.

'Perkiades?'

'Bank,' said Mr Fehmi.

'I have him already,' said Georgiades.

'He's all right,' said Mr Fehmi. 'He works for the Bank.'

'Does that make him all right?' asked Georgiades.

Mr Fehmi smiled.

Georgiades went on to the next page. Every time he made a note, Mr Fehmi clicked his fingers and his minion recorded it too.

'You are noting the crossings-out?'

'Of course!' said Georgiades, wide-eyed.

'Mere accidents,' said Mr Fehmi, a little sharply.

'Perhaps,' said Georgiades.

'Any references to Jabir?' asked Owen.

Georgiades nodded.

'Twice. Just the name. Written separately, not with the others. Occurs once with another name but it's a bit separate and could be chance.'

'What's the name?'

'Tufa.'

Mr Fehmi clicked his fingers.

Georgiades came to the end of the entries and looked up.

'Not much there,' he said.

'Only what you would expect,' said Mr Fehmi softly.

'Then why was it taken?' asked Owen.

Mr Fehmi raised eyebrows.

'Taken?'

'*Entre nous.*'

'Ah!' Mr Fehmi smiled and brushed the matter aside with his hand. 'Are you not expecting too much?' he asked. 'A young man commits suicide. Personal pressure. Family pressure, perhaps. Would that appear in his diary? His Appointments Diary?'

'If they were work pressures, perhaps.'

Mr Fehmi gestured towards the diary.

'Not much evidence of that, surely? Of course, it's only appointments that appear in the diary. We don't know what he did with the rest of his time. But, somehow, I do not get the impression that Mr Fingari was collapsing from overwork.'

'There are different kinds of pressure. Perhaps it was one big thing that he was worried about.'

'Perhaps. But would you find evidence of that in his diary?'

'There's a lot of appointments to do with the Agricultural Bank,' said Georgiades.

'Is that surprising? It was an important part of his work. But perhaps you're right, Captain Owen. Maybe he was worried about that. It was the first time he had worked on anything as big. It would not be surprising. But . . .'

He stopped and spread his hands.

'If you're right, Captain Owen, why continue the prying? A young man. Heavy responsibility for the first time. Difficulties, perhaps. Conscientious. Worries about it. It gets on top of him. Sad, tragic, the Department should ask itself questions. But do we need to go into it any more, Captain Owen? Why pry? Cannot we just leave it at that?'

'We could,' said Owen, 'were it not for the diary. Why was it taken?'

'I have a suggestion about that,' said Mr Fehmi.

'Yes.'

'Prudence. Excessive, misguided prudence. Just that.'

*

'I never like these office jobs,' complained Georgiades as they left together. 'I never feel I get the hang of what's really going on. They go about things in a different way. I've got these names, right? I'll take them away and check them out. But that's not the way they'd go about it.'

'No?'

'No. What they would do is put them into the files. Or something. That's what we ought to be doing.'

'Checking them against the files? Well, why not?'

'I'll tell you why not,' said Georgiades late the next day, pushing away the file in front of him. 'Because it makes my head ache, because I'm not getting anywhere, because I feel as if I'm in a quicksand, sinking, sinking. The sand is up to here!' He clutched his throat dramatically. 'Here!' he clasped his hand to his mouth. 'Here!' He held his hand above his head and pounded his head heavily with the other. He began to cough and splutter.

'For God's sake!' said Owen, and fetched him a glass of water.

'Well, are you getting anywhere?' Georgiades challenged.

'Not really,' Owen admitted. 'I can tie names to particular parts of the Agricultural Bank stuff but I don't know that that gets us much further. This chap Perkiades, for example, appears to be concerned with debt collection. This chap Iskander is something to do with capital bids. But what does that tell us?'

'Exactly!' said Georgiades. 'It tells us nothing. And you know why? It's because we don't think like them. We're normal, decent people. We go home at the end of the day and love our wives. These blokes don't. They just stay here, working—'

'Fingari wasn't like that,' Owen objected.

'He was just a beginner. He'd have soon learned. No, I tell you what it is. We're the wrong blokes to be doing this sort of thing. You need somebody who thinks like them, you need somebody like—'

He stopped. His eyes met Owen's

'Well, it takes one to catch one, doesn't it?'

CHAPTER 8

Nikos, once he had recovered from the shock of being asked to set foot outside the Bab el Khalk, was like a fish in water.

He approached the office in a quite different way from Owen and Georgiades. For them there was the action then there was the recording of it. The recording went into the files so what the files were, essentially, was history.

For Nikos, the files were part of the action. They fed into the flows of which, at bottom, the office was constituted.

Nikos saw everything in terms of flows. The first thing he did when he sat down at Osman Fingari's desk was to call for the office clerk.

'Reconstitute Fingari's in-tray,' he commanded.

'It has been redistributed,' said the clerk snootily.

'You can redistribute it afterwards,' said Nikos.

Next, he wanted to see all the papers that had passed through Fingari's in-tray since he had joined the office.

'All?' gasped the clerk.

'All,' said Nikos, settling himself more firmly in Osman Fingari's chair.

The clerk swallowed. 'It will take time,' he said weakly.

'Not too much time,' snapped Nikos, relishing his new role. In the Bab el Khalk he did not often get the opportunity to exercise absolute power.

The files began to accumulate on Nikos's desk. Owen was surprised to see how many there were.

'That is because the paper comes in and the paper goes out,' said Nikos. 'Only the exceptional thing is kept in Fingari's own files: the things he was working on, perhaps.'

'Like the Agricultural Bank?'

Nikos nodded.

'Anything he'd finished working on would have been passed out. And that would include most of the routine stuff that he handled.'

The routine stuff was such things as applications for grants for land improvement, requests to register change of land use, complaints about water rights, notification of work required on levees, the high banks which enclosed the river and prevented flooding, orders to village headmen to undertake necessary repairs to local irrigation systems and so on.

Owen was impressed at the volume; Nikos wasn't.

'Take him five minutes,' he sniffed. He picked up a grant application.

'See this? All he'd do would be glance at it, initial it and pass it on. One minute if he read slowly.'

'What about that initialling? Would it be enough to authorize payment?'

'Yes. But look at the size of the sum.'

Three pounds.

'No one's going to get rich on that, if that's what you were thinking,' said Nikos. 'He'd only have limited signing authority. Anything big would have to go higher up.'

He rummaged through the files and produced a request to register change of land use.

'Now this,' he said, 'is what they really have to watch. Somebody owns some land. It's poor quality land, which in this country means it's been assessed as unsuitable for growing cotton on. Change the assessment and the land value rockets immediately.'

'Who does the assessing?'

'A surveyor. But if you pay him enough you can get a surveyor to say anything. It's the approval of the assessment that's significant.'

'And that's done by—?'

'The Ministry. It used to be done by the Land Commission but the volume of applications became so great—everyone in the country started trying it on—that they passed it to the Ministry.'

'Do they have the expertise?' asked Owen, thinking of the difference between the Department of Agriculture and the Khedivial Agricultural Society.

'You don't need expertise. Somebody owns a bit of desert. One day it rains, for the first time in a hundred years, and the next morning they're at the Ministry asking for the land to be classified as permanently irrigated! Ninety per cent of the claims can be turned down automatically. But it still needs someone senior to turn them down.'

'And that's why it would come to Fingari?'

Nikos nodded.

'And why it takes him only a couple of minutes.'

Owen felt, however, slightly relieved, both from Osman Fingari's point of view and for the sake of the Ministry, that at least he had something to do.

Apart, that was, from what he did for the Agricultural Bank.

'Will you stop jumping up and down like a yo-yo?' Owen complained.

This time, however, Paul was gone for a long time, so long that Owen decided he was not coming back and passed the contents of his glass into his own. Whereupon Paul, of course, came back.

He saw his empty glass and stopped, astounded.

'Even here?'

Owen hastily signalled to the waiter.

'Even here what?'

'The liquidity base is shrinking. Or, as I suspect, the liquidity is shrinking and the base is taking over.'

'What's going on?' asked Owen. 'Why are you rushing away all the time?'

'It's what I told you: cotton prices and all that.'

'You'd better explain. I need to know how the Agricultural Bank fits in.'

'Banks! I've had it up to here with banks lately. To start with, they work the wrong hours. Whenever you go along they're closed and whenever you go to bed they start working. It's all wrong. And do you know what's at the bottom of it?'

He sipped his glass and then, remembering that he might be called away at any minute, took another sip.

'Modernization!' he said.

'What's that got to do with it?'

'It's all these damned cables lying along the bottom of the ocean. Very dangerous, and not just for those unfortunate enough to be down there, the fish and the crabs and the lugs and so forth, but even for the rest of us up here. It's all telegrams these days. You can't get a decent gap between crises. Governments are crumbling because of it.'

A telephone rang. Paul flinched and hastily took another sip. It was not for him, this time, however.

'The banks are the worst,' he said. 'Especially right now. The cables are coming all the time.'

'What are they coming *about*?'

'Money, lack of; lending, too much of; borrowing, too much of. Belts needing to tighten. Bootlaces you need to pull yourself up by. I do find it provoking when banks take on this moral tune. It's bad enough in church or in the Assembly. Coming from banks it's, well, I was going to say, a bit rich, but that's the one thing they claim they're not.'

'Paul. I need to know about the Agricultural Bank.'

'The same as all the other banks: lent more than it's got. Most of what it's got it's borrowed from somebody else.

The trouble is that, with the general squeeze, the somebody else wants it back now.'

'Who's the somebody else?'

'Other banks. Here and abroad. Hence the cables.'

'Who *owns* the Agricultural Bank?'

'You do.'

'Oh no, now come on—'

'I do. We all do. The Government does.'

'You mean Zokosis, Singleby Stokes, that bunch of tricksters, work for the Government?'

'The Government set it up. They manage it.'

'They report to a Minister?'

'Ah no. Well, perhaps at arm's length. The length of the arm is particularly important because the Bank has to raise money in order to lend it to other people, it raises it from other banks, and banks trust banks and not governments. Why, I don't know, unless it is that they trust them more not to ask questions and not complain about charges.'

'They don't seem to trust Zokosis and crew,' objected Owen. 'Not over this new loan, at any rate. They want a guarantee from the Ministry of Agriculture.'

'Just at the moment,' said Paul, 'it's a question of finding someone with the capacity to foot the bill. And financiers are always prepared to trust governments for that!'

'I'm surprised the Government is even faintly interested.'

Paul stared at him.

'Don't you realize?' he said. 'The whole of Egyptian agriculture is tied to the Bank. If the Bank goes under, so does just about everything else.'

'It's crazy to let yourself be put in that situation.'

'It may seem crazy now,' Paul admitted, 'but when it was set up it was actually a very good idea. The fellahin had got so in debt to local moneylenders that the whole system was in danger of collapsing. The Bank was set up to make loans to small farmers at low rates of interest. It worked, too, until the recession came along.'

'You think the Bank's a good thing.'

'I certainly do.'

'The opposition don't.'

'Sidki and Abdul Aziz? They're all in favour of lending the fellahin money. What's upset them is that the Bank's started calling loans in.'

'They don't like this deal with the Ministry over a guarantee.'

'If the Bank doesn't get that,' said Paul, 'it's going to be calling in a lot more loans, I can tell you.'

Barclay was waiting for Owen in a Lebanese restaurant just off the Clot Bey. He was sitting at an outside table and there was a young Egyptian with him.

'You remember Selim?'

Owen recognized the architect who had been working on the restoration of the blue-tiled mosque the day they had visited it.

'He's the one who put me on to it.'

Grim-faced, Barclay led them through the tiny streets towards the Derb Aiah. Owen thought he recognized some of the places. Was not that the mosque itself just over there? Behind the houses? But the buildings pressed in, the heavy meshrebiya windows closed above him all aspect, even all light, was lost.

It came as something of a relief when they emerged into a small square and saw the sky above them once again. There were some delightful old buildings in the square. One of them was so like the mosque that for a moment Owen was puzzled.

'Surely—?'

'No, no,' said Barclay. 'It's a *hammam*.'

A public bath house. But not unlike a small mosque. The façade was ancient and faced with the same blue tiles as the mosque had been. The design was not as intricate, the tiles not quite as gem-like. They did not collect the light and sparkle as those on the mosque had done. But to Owen's untutored eye the buildings were of the same period and in the same spirit.

When he came close, however, he could see that it was a *hammam*. The entrance was narrow and sunk below ground level. And a towel was hung across the door, which indicated that it was being used by women.

Barclay led him past, turned abruptly up a side-street and then turned again so that they were, Owen judged, now behind the *hammam* and facing a tall derelict building.

The smell hit Owen even before he got inside. It was an indescribable compound of rotting cabbage, sulphur, excrement and animal corruption. It was so awful that Owen could hardly breathe. He put his hand up over his mouth.

'Sorry, old man,' said Barclay, 'but you'd better see it.'

It was not very easy to see anything. At the far end, however, some daylight came down what might have been stairs and when their eyes grew accustomed to the gloom they edged towards it.

Edged, because at every step their feet sank into something soft and rotten and foul, in which there were occasional little pieces of what felt like wire, which caught at them and threatened to trip them.

The stairs at the end were not quite stairs because they were packed solid with the same sort of rotting material, so that they formed an upward plane rather than stairs.

They went up and came out in the room alone. It had no roof, which accounted for the light. They could now see properly.

The room was packed feet-deep with rubbish. There was household waste, green leaves, faded flowers, the offal of poultry and rabbits, broken pots and pans, rags and tatters of all kinds, peelings.

In one corner of the room the rubbish appeared to be

moving. And then Owen saw that there were dozens of cats, all tearing at something.

A man came into the room with a wheelbarrow and tipped out some more rubbish.

'What the hell is this?' said Owen.

Barclay led him on. In the next room some goats were picking over the rubbish and there were more cats. Crouched down in the ordure were some legless beggars feeling over the slime.

There was room upon room of rubbish and still the men were bringing more in. Some of the rooms were already full to shoulder height.

The wall of one of the upper rooms had crumbled away and gave on to the roofs around. They went across to it and looked out. Immediately below, right next to them, was a series of domes from which puffs of steam were emerging.

'It's the baths,' said Barclay.

There were strange objects lying on top of the domes and it took Owen a moment to realize that they were cats. There were scores of them, stretched out, enjoying the warmth which came up from the baths below.

There were also heaps of rags.

One of the heaps got to its feet. It was a small boy, who greeted Owen warmly.

'Effendi! We meet again! It is I, Ali!'

'Ali?'

'I arrange your meetings with Aisha.'

'What?' said Barclay.

'It's nothing,' said Owen hastily.

Ali came and took Owen by the hand.

'Do you want a look?'

'Look?'

Ali gestured towards the domes.

'You can look down through the holes where the steam comes out,' he said. 'You get quite a good view. Try this one! There's a girl just down there . . .'

'Thank you, Ali,' said Owen firmly. 'No!'

A man, hearing voices, came up some stairs on the other side of the domes. He shouted indignantly.

Several of the heaps of rags jumped up and ran off.

The man shook his fist at them.

'Those boys!' he said furiously. 'Always at it!'

He saw the men through the wall and looked at them curiously.

'A word with you,' said Barclay.

The man climbed out on to the roof and walked across. 'Effendi?'

'This,' said Barclay, almost unable to speak. 'All this!' He waved his hand at all the rubbish.

'Keep me going for a long time,' said the man.

'It's foul!'

The man shrugged. 'It's handy,' he said. 'It's not so easy to get wood these days. And by the time it's got to you, it's not cheap, either. Now this stuff, well, it's not agreeable, I know, but it burns like wood and it's a lot cheaper.'

'You run your boilers on this?' asked Owen.

'That's right. Fifty-six cartloads a month I take.'

'That's a lot of cartloads.'

'We use a lot of fuel.'

'There are more than fifty-six cartloads here,' said Selim suddenly.

'I like to think ahead,' said the man.

'You used to take fifty-six cartloads,' said Selim. 'Now you're taking hundreds. Why?'

'I told you. I like to think ahead.'

'Why have you suddenly started thinking ahead?'

'I've not suddenly started—' The man stopped and looked at Selim suspiciously. 'Here,' he said, 'what has it got to do with you?'

'It's disgusting,' said Barclay, 'and an extremely serious threat to people's health in the neighbourhood.'

The man shrugged again. 'They've got used to it, effendi. It won't do them any harm.'

'What about the baker's next door?' asked Selim.

'Look,' said the man. 'I've got to make a living the same as he has. If he doesn't like what I do, he can get out. And that,' he said pointedly to Selim, 'goes for other people, too.'

He shuffled back across the hot domes, kicking some of the cats out of the way. They came back again as soon as he had disappeared down the stairs. So did the boys.

Barclay took Owen back down into the street.

'Well, you've seen it,' he said.

'Yes. I've seen it. But—?'

He had seen such sights before. They no longer shocked him.

'There's not much I can do about it,' he said. 'Try Public Health.'

Barclay shook his head.

'No, no,' he said. 'It's not that.'

He looked at Selim.

'It's an old trick,' said Selim, 'if you want to get some-body out of a place. You make it unpleasant for them to stay.'

'The rubbish, you mean?'

'Yes. Someone's paying him to pile it up. He thinks he's come into a fortune! He doesn't realize his turn will come.'

'What are you saying?'

'It's your friend again, the developer,' said Barclay. 'Only it's not *waqfs* this time.'

'I've looked at the map,' said Selim. 'Mr Barclay has told me about the *waqfs*. I thought I would check on the properties affected. They're in a straight line.'

'The road?'

Selim nodded.

'I'm sorry,' said Owen. 'I don't understand. Which build-ing is it this time?'

'The baker's. It's right next to the *hammam*. Get that, get these houses behind the *hammam*, they're all derelict—in fact, he's probably already got them—take in the *hammam* itself, and what you've got is a whole big area.'

'Why does he have to go to these lengths? Won't the baker just sell?'

'The baker doesn't want to sell. He's always lived here. The trouble is, business is being affected.'

'By the smell?'

Owen was sceptical. He thought Cairenes had a high tolerance for such things.

'By the flies, the maggots. Even the Cairenes notice things like that,' said Selim drily, guessing what Owen was thinking.

They went round to the front of the *hammam*. The baker's shop was tucked down one side. Perhaps they had even shared sources of heat at one time. The entrance, like that of the *hammam*, was below ground and a constant stream of small boys was coming out.

They all held their arms out sideways, as if they had been crucified. Each arm was looped with bread. Egyptian bakers made their bread in rings which hung conveniently over an arm.

One of the boys gave a pirouette as he passed.

'Effendi!'

'You again!' said Owen, recognizing the monstrous Ali.

Inside the shop the baker was talking to some of his customers. Owen recognized one of these, too: his friend, the barber.

'You must resist, Mustapha!' he was saying vehemently to the baker.

'I would,' said the baker, 'I would! But what about these?'

He waved an arm at his customers.

'We will resist, too,' said one of them stoutly.

'We must get together!' said the barber.

'I'm all for that!' said the baker. 'Though I don't think it will do much good.'

'It will,' said the barber. 'You see!'

'It's no good,' said the baker. 'We're up against the big boys.'

'They can be beaten!'

The baker looked sceptical.

'In the end,' he said, 'it all comes down to power. And they've got it and we haven't.'

'We have powerful friends, too,' said the barber.

'Oh yes?' said the baker. 'Speak for yourself!'

'The Widow Shawquat has, at any rate.'

'The Widow Shawquat?'

'Yes.'

'What friends?' the baker scoffed. 'Hamid the Deaf?'

'The Mamur Zapt.'

'Very likely,' said the baker.

'And here he is!' said the barber, catching sight of Owen in the doorway.

As soon as he decently could, Owen extricated himself. There was no point in raising hopes he could not fulfil. There had been too much of that with the Widow Shawquat. He had allowed himself to be inveighled into promising help which he probably couldn't give.

He was beginning to wish now that he hadn't responded to her letter, or that he had responded in a more guarded way. Nikos was probably right. The Mamur Zapt's Box was a thing of the past. It might have been all right two hundred years ago when the Mamur Zapt had actually had power to do things and there was some point in getting in touch with him.

Now there was no point at all. He didn't have power to do things. All that sort of thing was handled by Ministries. OK, so they were unresponsive. That was not something he, Don Quixote Owen, could put right or compensate for.

Nikos was probably right. In order to be able to function at all, they probably had to put distance between themselves and the people they served.

See what a mess you got in if you wandered around! He would do much better to stay in his office like Nikos.

'Something ought to be done,' said Barclay.

Heavens, he was at it, too. He really ought to know better. He was in the Public Service himself, wasn't he?

'Maybe, but I'm not sure I'm the one who can do it.'

Barclay looked disappointed.

'Who is?' asked Selim.

'It's really a planning matter, isn't it?'

'We don't have the powers,' said Barclay dejectedly.

'In that case it's a matter for the politicians.'

'But you *are* the politicians!' said Selim.

'No, we're not!' said Owen and Barclay together.

'But—you're the ones who exercise power.'

'I don't know about that, old boy,' said Barclay. 'Not much power about where I'm sitting.'

Selim looked at Owen.

'Nor where I'm sitting, either.'

Selim made a gesture of helplessness.

'Forgive me,' he said, 'but I don't understand. I always thought—as an Egyptian—that the British controlled everything. Ministries have to do what they tell them. The Khedive is in their hands. The Army, the Police—'

Barclay looked at Owen.

'It doesn't quite work like that. There are—limits. We have to work with others. The Ministers—the Khedive, even—we don't just tell them what to do. We sort of— work at it between us.'

'But who, then, can stop the road?' Selim demanded.

'There has to be pressure,' said Owen, 'political pressure. That's what Government responds to.'

'Does it have to respond? Can't it take the initiative?'

'Heavens, no!' said Owen/Barclay. 'That's not the way things work!'

'By "political pressure", do you mean pressure from the Assembly?' asked Selim.

'Well . . .'

'I always thought no one took any notice of them at all.'

'Well, that's putting it a bit strongly—'

'Would it do any good? I know some politicians. I could—'

Owen remembered suddenly that Barclay had spoken of Selim as 'a bit political'. That might mean merely that Selim was, like most young educated Egyptians, sympathetic to the Nationalist movement. Or it might mean something more.

'I think you would need to be careful,' he said. 'Politicians use issues for their own purposes and it could recoil on you.'

Selim, however, looked determined.

'This has to be fought,' he said.

'Quite agree with you,' said Barclay.

'It's not just the mosque,' said Selim. 'It's the whole city.'

'If the road goes through, yes,' said Barclay.

'Oh, come!' said Owen. From the Widow Shawquat's school to the whole city was a bit of a far cry.

'It's true, though!' Selim insisted. 'Its whole character would be altered. The Old City as we know it would disappear. The effect would be to create a completely modern city. It would—'

The discussion continued over several cups of coffee in the Lebanese restaurant they'd met at earlier. The world of town planning was a new one and in Selim and Barclay Owen had met two enthusiasts. They described at length the tremendous things that might be done—and the terrible things that were likely to be done.

At last their volcanoes were exhausted.

'The trouble is,' said Barclay gloomily, 'Public Works isn't like that.'

'Nor the Ministry of *Waqfs*,' said Selim.

'A lot of good people come into the Department thinking it will be,' said Barclay, 'and then they're disappointed.'

'Was Fingari one of those?' asked Owen.

'Fingari?'

'He was one of yours, I think. Moved to Agriculture about six months ago.'

'Knew him well. No, not really. A bit . . .' Barclay hesitated. 'Well, careerist.'

'Osman Fingari?' asked Selim.

'Yes.' Barclay turned to him. 'On the finance side. You must have come across him.'

'Oh yes. I worked with him on the Bab-el-Azab developments.'

'Why do you ask?' said Barclay.

Owen told him about the suicide. Both men were shocked.

'This is terrible!' said Selim. 'I must go at once and pay my respects to the family.'

'You know them?'

'Not well. I saw a lot of Osman at that time, though.' He hesitated and seemed oddly embarrassed. 'Isn't there a sister?' he asked diffidently.

'There is. Aisha. I think she would be glad of a visit.'

'Very sad!' said Barclay, distressed. 'We never thought—'

'It seems to have happened rather suddenly. There were no signs when he was with you?'

Barclay shook his head.

'Not that I saw. Of course, with these things you never know.'

'Pressure?'

'I wouldn't have said so.' He turned to Selim. 'Did you notice anything?'

Selim thought, then shook his head.

'He was very involved in the Bab-el-Azab scheme,' he said. 'But I didn't see any signs that it was getting on top of him.'

'Political pressures?' asked Owen.

'Why political?' said Selim, suddenly wary.

'I thought all you bright young men wanted to change the world.'

'Save the world,' said Selim. 'Not change it.'

CHAPTER 9

The coffee-house was in the Ismailiya. Owen was a little surprised. The Ismailiya was the most Europeanized of the quarters and pricey enough to be out of the reach of the ordinary Egyptian effendi, or office-worker, even one of as exalted a rank as Osman Fingari.

'That,' said Georgiades, 'is precisely the point.'

Inside, the floor dropped down to a lower level, as in many Egyptian restaurants, and was arranged in alcoves, each with its separate brazier and coffee-pot. The lights were low and the furnishings soft. The carpet on the floor was about three inches deep. The fact that it was on the floor and not on the wall was a European touch.

Georgiades led him down to one of the alcoves and looked around benignly. A waiter came forward, stirred the charcoal in the brazier and settled the coffee-pot more securely.

'Who's paying for this?' asked Owen.

'Don't be like that,' protested Georgiades. 'This is work. Enjoy it while you can.'

Some men were singing in a neighbouring alcove. They were singing sentimental Arab love songs. At the end of each verse they burst into maudlin applause. It never ceased to astonish Owen that Egyptians seemed to manage to get drunk purely on coffee.

'This is where Jabir used to bring him,' said Georgiades.

'I thought Aisha said he came home drunk? Really drunk, I mean.'

'Maybe they went on to a bar afterwards. Or maybe he had enough at lunch-time to last for the rest of the day. Anyway, this is where he used to come in the evenings.'

'Who used to pay?'

'Jesus, this is becoming an obsession with you!'

'No, no. I only meant that it would be a lot for him.'

'I don't think he used to pay.'

'Jabir?'

'And others. They were all pretty rich.'

'The trouble is,' said Owen, 'that even if he did pay, I can't see him getting sufficiently into debt to want to kill himself. Not on coffee-bills. Did they do anything else? Gamble?'

'Not here. And not, I think, much if at all anywhere else. They just talked.'

'Talked?'

'Well, you know young men . . .'

'Coffee? Talk? This is a den of vice!'

And yet he knew that was how most young effendis spent their evenings. They walked out with their friends, often their colleagues, in their smart dark suits and their red tasselled tarbooshes, and often with canes, short walking canes, and congregated in the cafés and drank coffee.

'It's not so much what he did as who he was with,' said Georgiades. 'These youngsters are rich. Pashas' sons. Jabir is, well, not a son but the cousin of a son. Fingari must have thought he'd really arrived.'

'And that Jabir was doing it as a favour?'

Georgiades gave him a side-long look. 'Well . . .' he said.

'He knew,' said Owen. 'He knew he was expected to give something in return. The question is what that was.'

'Why did Jabir take up with him again? Because he was now in a position where he could return favours. That means the Ministry.'

'It's the Ministry of Agriculture, which doesn't seem a likely place for doing people favours. Unless you're a farmer.'

'Or a rich, land-owing Pasha?'

One of the young men in the adjoining alcove got to his feet and staggered towards the toilet.

'Are you sure they're only drinking coffee?'

Georgiades beckoned the waiter.

'I feel terrible,' he said, 'drained! It's the work I've been doing, all that thinking. Even this excellent coffee is not doing the trick. Do you think you could pep it up with something?'

'A little cognac, effendi?' suggested the waiter.

'That would do fine. Make it a big one.' He looked at Owen. 'I'm only doing it in the cause of duty, you know.'

'Well, that explains the merriment. And perhaps why Fingari came home the way he did?'

The waiter returned and poured something into Georgiades's cup.

'The heat will release the aromas, effendi,' he said.

Georgiades sat back and sniffed.

'I think I'm catching them,' he said happily.

'Who does Jabir work for?' said Owen.

'Does the Trans-Levant Trading Bank mean anything to you?'

'No.'

'The name Kifouri?'

'Kifouri?'

Georgiades waited.

'Yes, it does,' said Owen slowly. 'He was one of the businessmen who approached me about Fingari. There were three of them. Zokosis, Kifouri and an Egyptian named Khalil. I thought he worked for the Agricultural Bank.'

'No. Not formally at any rate. He's not on the Board. He works for this other bank. Jabir seems to report to him.'

'Seems to?'

'Jabir doesn't officially work for the bank. He meets Kifouri regularly, though. They have lunch together. You remember Fingari's friends who used to lunch at that Greek restaurant? I got to know one of them —we had lunch together, as a matter of fact—and he pointed them out to me.'

'So you think Jabir might be working for Kifouri on this?'

'He might. There are other possibilities. He doesn't work for anyone all the time. He doesn't have a regular job at all. He stays on the fringe of things and, well, fixes. That's his job. He's a fixer.'

'Who else does he fix for?'

'His uncle, principally, Ali Reza Pasha. He's a business-man with interests in sugar, gum and property.'

'And cotton?'

'He has estates in the Delta.'

'So he *might* have an interest in the Ministry of Agri-culture?'

'He might. I've asked Nikos to see if there's anything in Fingari's files.'

'It would be interesting to know if he's got anything to do with that deal we can find out so little about. Anything that connects him with the Agricultural Bank?'

'Not directly. But he knows Jabir, who knows Kifouri, who knows Zokosis. Does that count?'

'Who knows me,' said Owen. 'Does that?'

'Nothing!' said Nikos. 'His name doesn't appear at all.'

'That may only mean,' said Georgiades, 'that he prefers to work through people like Jabir and Kifouri.'

'There are an awful lot of names that don't appear,' said

Owen, 'especially in connection with the Agricultural Bank. I was hoping Fingari's lunches might throw some of them up.'

'I've been through all the names,' said Georgiades, 'and they're all officials or directors or sidekicks of directors of the Agricultural Bank. All quite proper.'

'Fingari worries me,' said Owen. 'He drinks coffee, chats with the boys and goes home in the evenings; he goes out for lunches but they're always working ones. This decent life is sickening.'

'It's always the quiet ones who commit suicide,' said Georgiades.

'You're going to tell me next that, appearances to the contrary, he was working so hard that things genuinely could have got on top of him.'

'Well . . .' Nikos spread his hands.

'And yet somehow, in that decent, God-fearing life, he acquired, on a civil servant's pay, enough money to refurbish his house on a grand scale!'

Georgiades perched himself on Nikos's, that is, Osman Fingari's, desk.

'The deal with the Agricultural Bank is still in the offing,' he said, frowning. 'It wasn't concluded by the time he died. So the money wouldn't have been for that.'

'It was for something else,' said Nikos, 'to whet his appetite.'

'The money started coming,' said Owen, 'after he resumed his acquaintance with Jabir.'

'Which brings us back to the Pasha. Perhaps. He would only be interested in something big. Like this Agricultural Bank deal. Could he be going to lend the money himself, do you think?'

'No,' said Georgiades instantly. 'Pashas don't lend money. They borrow money. They never have it themselves.'

'All right. So who was going to lend it? That bank you were talking about?'

'The Trans-Levant?' Georgiades shook his head. 'Too small.'

'In my experience,' said Nikos, 'banks are like Pashas; they never have money themselves, they always borrow it. From other banks.'

'So somewhere in this chain, Ali Reza stands to make a lot of money. How? Through commission? What for? Setting it up? Through others?'

'There's nothing to connect him directly to Osman Fingari,' said Nikos.

'Nor to the Agricultural Bank. Where does he come in?'

'It's not in the files,' said Nikos. 'I've been through them all now. I've checked all the names Georgiades gave me. All those people he had lunch with. There's nothing which doesn't quite properly have their name on.'

'And nothing else which, well, raises any questions?' asked Owen.

Nikos shook his head.

'Not that I have been able to discover. It's all either Agricultural Bank working papers or ordinary office routine. The working papers, apart from some drafts he was working on, are all papers in normal Board circulation, that is, as public as these things usually are. The routine stuff is—well, routine.'

'So you've not got anywhere?' asked Georgiades.

'You could say that,' Nikos admitted. It was not like him to be so humble. 'Except . . .'

'Except?'

He laid a file on the desk before Owen.

'You wanted to know about Tufa,' he said.

'Tufa?'

'Fingari's diary,' said Georgiades. 'His name was on the page with Jabir.'

'Only it's not *his* name,' said Nikos. 'It's the name of a place.'

He opened the file. Inside was a single sheet of paper, an application to register a change of land use.

'It's the name of the village where the land is.'

Owen read through the application.

The parcel of land referred to was some distance away from the village of Tufa and had previously been classified as waste land of poor quality, suitable only for industrial use. The extension of a neighbouring irrigation scheme, however, had brought the possibility of regular supplies of water and raised the prospect of using the land for cultivation. The application was for the land to be regraded as suitable for first class agricultural use.

Owen looked at it blankly.

'What's this got to do with Jabir?'

'On the face of it, nothing,' said Nikos. 'But he presented the case for the application. There is a record of a meeting at which he was present.'

Owen turned the page over.

'I've checked all the details,' said Nikos. 'Everything is as it says. Look, here's the Water Board certificate.'

Which was, presumably, why Osman Fingari has signed his name neatly in the box marked 'Approval'.

'Zeinab? My dear boy, I'm delighted!' said Nuri Pasha. 'Always wanted to marry her mother. Asked her lots of times. She wouldn't have it, though. A Pasha to marry a courtesan! She said it would damage my reputation. My dear, I said, you don't know my reputation!'

He chuckled and stretched his hand out for another thin cucumber sandwich. The suffragi standing behind him hastily moved round and edged the plate forward. He touched the silver teapot inquiringly.

'I think so,' said Nuri, 'I think so.'

Nuri, a great believer in things European, since the Europeans had come to control the country, was an enthusiast for English tea. He drank it, however, in the French way, without milk. English by adoption he might be; France, though, as with most of the Egyptian upper class, was ingrained in him.

He sat back in his chair.

'A beautiful woman, you know!'

His eyes looked wistfully out over the immaculately kept flowerbeds as if there, in the distance, in the rose garden, perhaps, or among the bougainvillæa, he might still hope to see her. His intoxicated pursuit of her had been one of the great court scandals of thirty years before.

'Zeinab takes after her, of course.'

A frown came over his face.

'In some ways, that is. Beautiful figure, beautiful. A real credit to her mother. A little on the thin side, perhaps, but then, I always like them thin. Unusual, that. Egyptians like them fat. More to get hold of, I suppose. But not me, no.'

He frowned again.

'It's the face, though.'

'Oh, come,' said Owen, moved to protest on behalf of his beloved.

'A real Bedawin face. Don't know where that comes from. Not her mother, who had a most delicate, soft, round face. My grandmother, I think. It was always said that my great-grandfather had taken a Bedawin. Well, it's all right, I suppose, only the face comes out like a hawk.'

Nuri helped himself to another sandwich and considered the matter.

'Plenty of fire, of course. That goes with it. I like a girl with spirit. Her mother had that, of course. My goodness, yes!'

It was said, indeed, and not just by Zeinab, who made the point regularly to Owen, that the real reason why Zeinab's mother had refused Nuri was that she wished to keep her independence.

To do him justice, it was a reason that Nuri might have appreciated. He certainly appreciated it in Zeinab, allowing his daughter a licence which was as great an affront to polite society as his devotion to her mother had been.

'Mother *and* grandmother,' decided Nuri. 'Both sides. That explains it. But as to money,' he said, darting a sudden swift look at Owen which had everything of the hawk in it and nothing of the soft and delicate, 'that, my boy, is a bit difficult. '

He shifted himself in his chair. The suffragi, correctly interpreting a change of mood, hastily passed Nuri another cup of tea and did not offer to do the same for Owen.

'The fact is,' continued Nuri, 'that I have a few problems myself just at the moment. The cotton crop, you know. The idle scoundrels on my estates have let the seed deteriorate. Yes—' he looked at Owen with a frown—'deteriorate. The yield has fallen off to the point at which I am seriously considering whether I can afford to go to Cannes this year.'

'Sorry to hear that.'

'Well, it *is* unfortunate. I was particularly hoping to meet a friend, a lady, in fact, an American lady, you might know her—' Owen did know her—'and she has somewhat expensive tastes.'

'That's, actually, rather the situation with Zeinab.'

'But my dear fellow,' said Nuri, shocked, 'you wouldn't want her to be content with the second-rate. That's not her at all.'

'No, it certainly isn't. But the problem is finding the money.'

'Exactly!' cried Nuri, pounding his knee. 'You've described my problem exactly!'

The suffragi, relieved that things were going better, poured them both cups of tea. Owen's, however, tasted bitter.

'My pay, you see, as a captain—'

'Pitiful. I've said so to the Khedive himself. Government service is grossly underpaid, I said. It's putting temptation in their way.'

'Yes, but—'

'It was when I had just become a Minister myself. You can't expect me to become rich on this, I said! But, of course, I hadn't understood. An old friend took me aside afterwards. My dear chap, he said, you're thinking about it in quite the wrong way. You're seeing it, forgive me, rather as a workman does: for so much work one gets so much pay. But that's not the way to see it all.'

'No?'

'No. You should look upon it not as a job but as an investment. It's not the pay you get—that, forgive me, is rather a low way of seeing it—it's the use you can make of it. And the joy of a minister's job is that there's quite a lot of use you can make of it. If only,' said Nuri gloomily, 'I were a minister now!'

'Yes, but—'

Nuri leaned forward and patted him on the knee.

'It's not the pay, dear boy. You'll never become rich that way. It's what you make of the job. Think of it as an opportunity. Now, surely, as Mamur Zapt you are extremely well placed '

'How did it go?' asked Zeinab.

'Not very well,' Owen admitted. 'He said he was short of cash himself.'

'He probably is. It's those dreadful people on his estate who have planted the wrong seed.'

'Seed?' said Owen, sitting up.

Zeinab pulled him down again.

'For goodness' sake!' she said. 'Now is not the time to take an interest in agriculture.'

Owen allowed himself to be pulled down.

'I was just thinking,' he said.

'You always are. Now stop worrying. I'm sure it will be all right in the end. You must be patient. He really is short of cash.'

'Yes, but when he's short he means a million. When I'm short I mean a couple of hundred.'

'You must try to bridge the gap, darling,' Zeinab advised. 'Spend more and then you will be short of a million, too.'

'With you to help me,' said Owen, 'that should be no problem.'

Zeinab wriggled herself into a more comfortable position without opening her eyes.

'You always seem to be thinking about money these days,' she complained. 'Can't you think about anything else?'

'As a matter of fact . . .' said Owen, easing himself across her.

'List of members?' said the Chairman, taken by surprise. 'Well, I don't know about that. We're rather an exclusive body, you know. There are members of the royal family. Prince Fuad, Prince Kamal—I'm sure they wouldn't wish . . .'

'In absolute confidence, of course.'

'Well, if it's in confidence, I suppose . .'

The Chairman fetched the list. It ran to many pages.

'For an exclusive body, you have a lot of members,' Owen observed.

'The cream,' said the Chairman, 'the cream!'

It was, indeed, the elite of Egypt. Royal Family, Ministers, Pashas, Members of the Assembly, senior members of the British Administration, eminent members of the business community—Singleby Stokes, for instance—bankers, diplomats, all were well represented.

Owen was amused to see that even Nuri's name appeared, although the flowers that Zeinab's father was interested in gathering were not normally of the horticultural variety. He was, however, assiduous at cultivating old relationships with those about the Khedive, never having quite abandoned hope that one day when the Khedive was constructing a Government he might still remember his old supporter.

There were various other Pashas in the list. Owen wrote down their names.

The Chairman looked worried. 'I say, old chap—'

'Just noting the names of fellow enthusiasts,' said Owen soothingly.

Among them was that of Ali Reza Pasha.

'Mr Chairman, I protest!' said Abdul Aziz Filmi.

'What, again?' murmured one of the representatives of the House Finance Committee. He caught his neighbour's eye and grimaced. The Chairman of the Bank of Egypt grimaced back. Egyptians and British were alike on this.

Paul looked at his watch.

'If you have to, Mr Filmi,' he said politely.

'I do. I cannot let this discussion proceed further without calling the meeting's attention to the impact such proposals would have on the fellahin.'

'We've been through all this, Mr Filmi,' said the Minister of Finance wearily.

'But you still haven't addressed the problem!' cried Mr Filmi, pounding his fist upon the table.

The Minister looked at him with distaste.

'We are not in the Chamber now, Mr Filmi,' he said coldly. 'Can we not dispense with the histrionics?'

'How else can I break through this wall of indifference? How else can I get you to pay attention to the needs of the people you are supposed to serve?'

'Offensive!' said someone on the other side of the room.

'It will hurt the fellahin a lot more if banks start going under,' observed one of the foreign bankers.

Mr Filmi turned on him.

'I agree. That is why I support the principle of an injection of funds into the banking system. What I am objecting to is the suggestion that existing loans be called in.'

'But, Mr Filmi,' said the banker, 'the banks are over-lent. If they don't do something about that it will be no good us injecting more money. It will be pouring good money after bad.'

'Tighten credit if you must!' declared Mr Filmi. 'But do not do so at the expense of the poorest!'

'We all have to share in the misery, Mr Filmi,' said the Minister, 'fellahin as well as Pasha.'

'The burden on the Pasha,' said Mr Filmi drily, 'is rather less.'

'I don't know about that,' said the Minister, himself a Pasha.

Owen wondered if he was a member of the Khedivial Agricultural Society. He took the list out of his pocket and studied it surreptitiously. He was.

Mr Filmi was now putting forward an argument that loans to fellahin should be considered differently.

'I thought Mr Filmi was opposed to special treatment for the Agricultural Bank,' said the Minister of Finance slyly.

'So I am!' said Mr Filmi, stung. 'That would, indeed, be a case of pouring good money after bad!'

'The Agricultural Bank? What's that?' asked one of the bankers.

'It's not a bank in your sense of the word,' said Paul. 'It's a Government Agency.'

The bankers looked doubtful.

'And under investigation by the Mamur Zapt,' put in Mr Filmi.

'Really?'

The bankers looked even more doubtful.

'A particular employee,' said the Minister. 'Not the bank in general.'

'How are you getting on?' asked Mr Filmi.

'I'm making progress,' said Owen.

'I think we should return to the general issue,' said Paul, 'which is the conditions on which our friends overseas would be prepared to make a substantial loan to the Egyptian Government.'

Unfortunately, friends overseas had already, on many occasions, made substantial loans to the Egyptian Government. The financial history of Egypt for the past thirty years consisted of substantial loans.

Somewhat to Owen's surprise, the friends seemed prepared to come up with money once again. He was less surprised when the rate of interest was mentioned.

The discussion became technical and his attention wandered. It came back again when he heard roads being mentioned.

'That would be a good example,' said the banker. 'We would always be willing to invest in specific projects. Providing they looked like being profitable, of course.'

'I don't see how blasting a road through the middle of Cairo would be profitable,' objected Paul. 'Rather the reverse!'

'There is tremendous potential for development in Cairo,' said the Minister eagerly, 'and of course, a prerequisite is the right infrastructure.'

'Of course!'

The bankers looked impressed.

'It would cost an arm and a leg,' said Paul.

'But think of the jobs it would create!' said the Minister.

'Millions!' said Paul. 'It would cost millions!'

'The price of modernization!' said the Minister.

The bankers looked even more impressed. Even Mr Filmi seemed sympathetic.

'The city would explode,' said Owen harshly.

'Civil unrest!' said Paul.

'Oh, I think that could be contained,' said the Minister.

The meeting closed soon afterwards. Owen had hoped to have a word with Paul. Instead, he was captured by Mr Filmi.

'You must stop it!' he said.

'I'll certainly do my best, but without stiffer planning machinery—'

'What are you talking about?' said Mr Filmi, bewildered.

'This road. Both roads. The effect on the city—'

Mr Filmi brushed it aside.

'I'm all in favour of development,' he said. 'Investment. Modernization. That's what this country needs.'

'But at the price of—?'

But Mr Filmi did not want to talk about that.

'No, no, my dear fellow,' he said, taking Owen by the arm. 'It's this deal with the Agricultural Bank. I understand that it's going ahead. You must stop it, my dear fellow, you must stop it!'

CHAPTER 10

Owen, however, was less interested in stopping the deal than he was in stopping the road; not so much for æsthetic reasons, persuasive though he had found the arguments of Barclay and Selim, nor out of loyalty to the Widow Shawquat, although he still meant to do what he could for her, but for reasons of state.

He saw the projected road as a major threat to order. The one through the Derb Aiah was bad enough but the one through the Old City was political dynamite. It would make some of the most conservative parts of the population explode in fury.

Any road built between the Bab-el-Futuh, and the Bab-el-Azab would inevitably mean the despoliation of a number of religious sites, including, almost certainly, the demolition of mosques. Some of these were among the most hallowed in the city and he could see no way in which an attempt to demolish them would not be resisted with blood.

Set against the command of religious loyalties, any loyalty the Khedive could call on was infinitesimal. He was seen as a foreigner anyway and, although Turkey was part of Islam, as part of a remote and secular power structure imposed from outside, a view reinforced by the fact that at the time of the nationalist Arabi uprising twenty years before the Khedive had had to call on British bayonets to maintain him in power.

And that was not all of it. Cairo was a city of many different nationalities and diverse religions. The road would also require the destruction of religious buildings other than Moslem ones. Copts, Greeks, Armenians, Montenegrins, Lebanese of all sects would be up in arms, not to mention the Protestants and Catholics.

It wasn't just one religious war that would be declared on the Khedive, it was dozens. And who would be called on to protect him? The British. The Minister had said unrest would be contained. Owen knew exactly who would be doing the containing.

Paul was working feverishly on the Consul-General and normally could be counted on to persuade him. It might be different this time, though, because of the financial crisis. If the banks were to lend money, they would be more likely to do so if they thought they would make a killing; and a major project of this sort offered opportunity for such a kill.

But while 'killing' was for them a metaphor, a business-man's way of talking, as Zokosis might have said, for Owen it was no metaphor. Killing was real; and therefore something to be avoided if you possibly could.

If anything was to be killed, it was the road; and the time to do that was before it even got started.

*

When Owen received the message from the Widow Shawquat—it came via the barber, a water-carrier who patrolled the city, his cousin who was an orderly at the Bab-el-Khalk, and a friend who made the tea in Owen's office, and was delivered orally—that she wished him to meet her sheikh, Owen was at first alarmed and then pleased.

He was at first alarmed because the sheikh would be a religious sheikh and he could see trouble ahead if the road got mixed up with religion. But then, on reflection, he was pleased. Here could be a person who might quite properly lodge an appeal against the *waqf* on the Widow's behalf.

When he met the sheikh, however, in the dark, airless room the Widow used for reception, he realized that this was out of the question. Anyone more likely to get himself tied up in the coils of Egyptian bureaucracy it was hard to imagine.

He was old and frail and half blind and his mental life was spent in a world different from his. His periods of lucidity enabled him to recognize his flock and give them spiritual counsel: but guidance on more worldly matters was not to be expected.

The Widow fussed over him and bossed him about, as she did all men. Owen could quite see how the sheikh had come to be enlisted on her side, although whether he understood what he was letting himself in for was another matter.

'The Mamur Zapt, eh? So you've got the ear of the Sultan. Well, just watch out!' he admonished the Widow. 'That way sin lies.'

The Widow was taken aback.

'Ask him for favours and he'll ask you for favours!'

The Widow giggled.

'Not much hope of that,' she said.

The sheikh continued to talk of the Sultan. Owen realized

after a while that he was harking back to a period even
before the Khedives.

He responded gently and sipped his coffee and ate his
sweet, sticky cake and wondered how soon he could decently leave.

The sheikh wiped his fingers on his galabeah and brushed
the crumbs from his mouth and then said, with a sudden
change of tone:

'Well, what about this *waqf*, then?'

Owen sat up with a jerk.

'It's a swindle,' said the sheikh. 'The Shawquats have
held that benefit for as long as I can remember. And *that*
goes back some time. I remember Ali Shawquat's grandfather—no, it wasn't his grandfather, it was his *great-*
grandfather—no, it wasn't—'

'It's always belonged to us,' said the Widow hastily, 'and
now it's been taken away.'

'It's got to be given back,' said the sheikh. 'It was given
for a purpose, and the purpose remains bright even though
those who now benefit be dulled.'

The Widow was not sure how to take this.

'We live in two worlds,' continued the sheikh. 'One is
the world of time, in which people come and go. The other
is a world in which the moral action is eternal. It is not for
us to attempt to put limits on it.'

'Quite right!' said the Widow. 'I think.'

'The recent decision must be reversed!'

'Yes, but—'

The sheikh banged his stick on the ground.

'I shall go to the Mufti,' he announced.

'God is great!' cried the Widow, enthusiastic but slightly
worried.

'He is indeed,' said Owen. 'But—the Mufti has much to
do. I wonder if it is as well to bother him with a thing like
this? Directly, I mean?'

The sheikh looked puzzled.

'What else does one do?' he asked.

Owen realized that he was back again in that old world in which the only way the lowly could get through to the great was by personal supplication. The only way in which you could get things done—Egypt had had three thousand years of bureaucracy—was by speaking to the boss yourself.

Or through an intermediary. Owen realized that was what the sheikh saw himself as called on to be.

The Widow Shawquat, however, was not one for intermediaries.

'But, Sheikh,' she said, 'you are frail. Can you manage on your own?'

'It is but the body that is frail,' said the sheikh, 'not the spirit.'

'It is, however, the body that I am worried about.'

The Widow looked at Owen anxiously. He could see what concerned her; not just the chance that the sheikh might collapse but also the not small probability that he might get it wrong.

But here she faced a dilemma. Custom, in a religious matter, precluded personal application by a woman; yet if she left it to someone else, she could not trust them to get it right.

It was probably this that had stopped her from letting the sheikh speak to the Mufti before. He had offered, Owen remembered, previously.

'I was wondering,' said the Widow, looking at him tentatively. Then—

'No!' he said, realizing what she was thinking.

'What?' asked the sheikh, bewildered.

The Widow took him by the arm.

'How could I let you go on your own, O Sheikh? What would they say of me? "She knew he was weak and frail, feeble and sick—"'

'I'm not sick!' protested the sheikh.

'"—and yet she let him go all that way on his own!"'

'It's only just down the road!'

'"Heartless woman, cruel woman!" That's what they would say. And they would be right. No,' she said, shaking her head firmly, 'I cannot let you do this for me.'

'Then, then what—?'

'Alone, that is,' said the Widow with emphasis. 'You must have one to support you.'

'Oh, all right,' said the sheikh testily, 'but who?'

The Widow looked at Owen.

'Would you mind?' asked Barclay.

Owen would. He felt he had spent enough time on the road already and still to come was the ridiculous visit to the Grand Mufti. He wasn't really getting anywhere with the Fingari business and ought to give it some attention. Then there was all the regular work which went through his office and which he had been neglecting. And to cap it all, Finance was querying one of his expenses claims.

So he did mind. But Barclay had been helpful to him and Selim seemed a reasonable chap and if they wanted to meet him about something, well, he could afford them a few minutes, he supposed.

They met at an open-air café.

'An apéritif?' suggested Barclay.

He and Owen each ordered a *pastis*. Selim had coffee. He seemed rather nervous today, fidgeting in his seat; although this might have been caused by the proximity of the shoeshine boys, who threatened to pounce at any moment.

Owen poured some water into his glass and watched the mixture cloud over.

'Well?' he said.

Barclay signalled to Selim to begin.

'I've spoken to my friends,' he said.

'His political friends,' Barclay put in.

'Yes?'

'They weren't interested,' said Selim gloomily. 'They were for the road, if anything.'

'Progress and development? Open the city up? Modernization?'

'Yes,' said Selim, surprised. 'How did you know?'

'I got the same story.'

'It's ridiculous to equate this with modernization,' said Barclay. 'Modernization doesn't have to mean—'

But Selim, who would normally have followed this hare with alacrity, just looked gloomily at Owen.

'What do we do now?' he said.

'It's not absolutely certain that it will be agreed. There are powerful voices against it.'

(Paul's).

'The trouble is,' said Barclay, 'that this time there are financial arguments *for* it.'

'It must not be decided purely on financial grounds,' Selim insisted. 'There are other considerations as well. Æsthetic, human.'

'They don't get you far in a place like Cairo, old man,' said Barclay unhappily.

'Can't we rouse public opinion somehow?' said Selim, addressing himself to Owen.

'It'll rouse public opinion all right if the road goes bang through the middle of the Old City,' said Owen sourly.

Selim gestured impatiently.

'It will be too late by then. What I wanted to ask you,' he said to Owen, 'was how would you feel if I sounded out public opinion in the area? Got a few people together to protest. Peacefully, of course.'

Owen opened his mouth. He was about to say that in his experience public protests in Cairo never ended peacefully, however they might start. In a city with so many divisions smouldering under the surface, religious, ethnic, political, discord on one thing was apt to ignite explosion over other things.

But then he closed his mouth again. One of the things he was always saying to the Consul-General and those in power—the Commander-in-Chief of the Army especially—was that not all protest is disorder. Was not this a case in point?

'You could always jump on it if things looked like getting out of hand,' said Barclay, watching him closely.

But could he? Would he be able to limit it if things went wrong? Experience shouted no. Once these things started you could never isolate them. People ran in from all sides to leap on the bandwagon and tilt it their way.

'If I could be sure other people wouldn't use it,' said Owen.

'I will do my best to see they don't,' said Selim.

'I know you will. But . . .'

The voice of experience was very loud in his ear.

'You see,' said Selim worriedly, 'I feel that ordinary people should have a voice in these things.'

'The people in the Derb Aiah,' said Owen tartly, thinking of the barber and the Widow Shawquat, 'have got plenty of voices.'

He stopped and looked at Selim.

'I could put you in touch with a few,' he said.

The good thing about a *pastis* is that it lasts a long time. Still more, two, or three, and they were still sitting there an hour later. By then their conversation had moved to other things.

'The thing that puzzles me,' said Owen, 'is why a developer should start at the Derb Aiah. It isn't even the road that's going to be built first. You'd have thought he'd have started with that one.'

'But he *has*,' said Selim, sitting up. 'You remember that Bab-el-Azab business?' he said to Barclay. 'Looking back, I can see now this would have been part of it.'

'What business is this?' asked Owen.

'Oh, it was one of those commissions that always irritates

you if you're an architect. I was asked to do some drawings
for a big project down by the Bab-el-Azab. I put a lot of
work in. I was paid all right, but the drawings were never
used. They were just there to accompany the planning
application.'

'What happened?'

'Nothing happened. That's just the point. It wasn't
meant to happen. The land is standing there idle. Waiting,
I now see, for the road.'

He turned to Barclay.

'That was how I first came across Fingari. He was handling the application for the Ministry. It was when he was
still at Public Works. I wasn't too pleased with him,
actually.'

'Why not?'

'Oh, he just messed around, delayed things. He didn't
ask the right questions and then he approved the thing on
the nod.'

'That was poor,' said Barclay. 'I didn't realize he was
like that. Of course, I only knew him when he was on the
finance side.'

'This was before then. He moved to accounts after.'

'Does the name Tufa mean anything to you?' asked
Owen.

They both shook their heads.

'Or the name Jabir?'

'Jabir?' said Selim thoughtfully. 'Wasn't he something to
do with a bank? I feel I may have come across him.'

'At the time of the Bab-el-Azab?'

'Perhaps. I don't remember now. I went to see the Fingaris the other day,' he said to Barclay, 'after Captain Owen
told me.'

'Did you meet Aisha?' asked Owen.

Selim blushed.

'Yes,' he said, 'as a matter of fact I did.'

*

Georgiades stopped in mock astonishment as he entered the office.

'Who is this man?' he asked. 'I seem to meet him everywhere I go in Cairo.'

Nikos looked up and scowled. He was still reeling from the experience. Twice! Twice in ten days he had had to leave the fastness of the Bab-el-Khalk and work in another office! And all of half a mile away, too!

'Did you find it?' asked Owen.

Nikos produced a file. It was exactly the same as the one he had shown them in Osman Fingari's office. There wasn't much difference between Ministries.

Owen opened it.

Tufa, he read again. Another application form. But this time an application to build. A cement factory or something, with workers' houses.

'What is all this?' he asked, bewildered.

'It's a planning application,' said Nikos. 'Because Tufa is still within the region, though outside of Cairo, it comes to Public Works.'

'Yes, but this is for a factory.'

'That's right. And therefore it goes to Public Works for approval.'

'Is this the same parcel of land?'

'Yes.'

'Nothing was mentioned about buildings on the other application.'

'There never were any buildings.'

'I don't get the point.'

'The application was made on the grounds that the land was waste and suitable only for industrial use. It was essentially desert land. The applicant was allowed to enclose it on condition that he used it for industrial purposes. It cost him virtually nothing.'

Georgiades began to laugh.

'And then he connects it up to an irrigation scheme and applies to register it as agricultural land?'

'That's right. And sells it without doing anything else to it. At a vastly enhanced price.'

'The buildings?'

'The plans were there merely to give an air of conviction to the application to enclose.'

'Never built?'

'Never intended to be built.'

'I've just heard of someone else doing this,' said Owen.

'And who did the plans go to?' asked Georgiades.

Nikos showed him the authorization box.

'Osman Fingari. Well! Both times.'

'Once when he was in the Ministry of Public Works. Once when he was in the Ministry of Agriculture.'

'Coincidence?'

Nikos smiled. 'What do you think?'

'Any mention of Jabir?'

'Presented the case again. His name doesn't appear in any of the paperwork. But again there are notes of the meeting.'

'Who was he presenting on behalf of?'

'It's a company. I think it's just a shell company. It doesn't seem to do any actual trading. But it's been used for things of this sort before.'

'At the Bab-el-Azab?'

'Yes,' said Nikos, surprised.

'Have you any idea who's behind it?'

'It's jointly owned. By the Trans-Levant Trading Bank and—'

'Yes?'

'A Mr Adli Naswas.'

'I wonder, Minister, if you could tell me how Mr Fingari came to be transferred to the Ministry of Agriculture?'

The Minister placed his hands on the top of the desk as if he were about to play a piano.

'A request in the ordinary way,' he said, 'I expect.'

'Who initiated the request?'

'Perhaps he did himself.'

'Did he?'

The Minister looked unhappy.

'I really cannot recall,' he said.

'You would have something in the files.'

'Yes.'

'May I see?'

The Minister hesitated, then rang the bell. An orderly appeared.

'Bring me the personal file of Osman Fingari,' he said. He turned back to Owen. 'Why do you ask?'

'I was surprised,' said Owen. 'You told me yourself that your Ministry was looked down on.'

'That is because it is new,' said the Minister, hurt.

'I'm sure. But then, you see, that makes it even more surprising. Mr Fingari was, I understand, very ambitious. Would he not have preferred a transfer to a major, established Department?'

The orderly brought the file.

'There seems to be no record of a personal request,' said the Minister.

'So I return to my question: who initiated the transfer?'

'I really cannot recall how it came about.'

The hands began to fidget.

'Was it initiated by Public Works?'

'I really cannot say.'

'I shall, of course, be able to find that out by other means.'

'Of course,' muttered the Minister.

'But I was wondering if the request had come from this Ministry?'

The Minister shook his head sharply.

'No,' he said, 'no. Definitely not.'

'I was wondering, you see,' said Owen, 'whether the request could possibly have originated from the person who was responsible for Mr Fingari's diary being removed?'

The hands froze.

'Was it removed? I thought it had been found? Yes, found in the office. Where it had been all the time.'

Owen smiled. And waited.

'I—I don't think the request originated from that person,' said the Minister after a while.

'No?'

'I I think it originated from someone higher up.'

'Even higher?'

The Minister nodded unhappily.

'You wouldn't like to tell me who?'

'I certainly would not.'

Owen considered for a moment or two.

'I wonder, then, if you could tell me anything about the *circumstances* of the request?'

'Circumstances?' said the Minister, puzzled.

'You received a request for Mr Fingari to be allowed to join your Department. Or perhaps he was simply posted to it?'

'Posted,' said the Minister.

'To specific duties?'

'Well, yes.'

'Isn't this unusual? Isn't it normally left to you to decide what duties a particular member of your staff performs?'

'Yes, but—'

'Yes?'

'There was the new link with the Agricultural Bank.'

'And you were told that Mr Fingari was to handle that?'

'Yes. He was assigned specifically for that purpose. So I was told.'

'I see. And, presumably, to negotiate the Agreement between the Department and the Bank?'

'That came up later. We didn't know about that at the time he joined us.'

'*You* didn't know about it,' said Owen.

The Minister flushed.

'Or did you?'

'No,' said the Minister vehemently. 'I did not.'

'Did they cut you in? Or,' said Owen cruelly, 'didn't they even bother?'

'I don't know what you mean.'

'Fingari was posted to your Department for a purpose,' said Owen. 'I just wondered if you were part of the purpose.'

The Minister breathed heavily.

'No,' he said, 'I was not.'

'Then why don't you tell me about it?' invited Owen.

The fingers drummed.

'I—I would,' the Minister said at last, 'but I don't really know anything. They kept it from me. I knew something was going on but I—I—'

'Didn't like to inquire too closely.'

The Minister was silent.

'You think I'm a weak man, don't you?' he said suddenly.

'Well—'

'And perhaps I am. But I am not corrupt. I would have stopped it if I could.'

'You still can.'

The Minister looked at him.

'How?'

'Announce—today, and with as much publicity as you can manage—that because of the doubts expressed about the new seed developed by the Khedivial Agricultural Society, the Ministry of Agriculture is arranging independent testing. Seeds have been sent to overseas laboratories for testing. Oh, and add that the project is being co-ordinated by Mr Aziz.'

'You think—?'

Owen rose.

'It will make you a hero,' he said.

'Yes,' said the Minister sourly, 'but probably a dead one.'

CHAPTER 11

There was uproar when the Minister's decision was announced. The telephones in the Ministry rang continuously
and there was an unbroken chain of orderlies bringing messages from other Ministries, the Assembly and the Consulate-General. Questions were asked in the House, and a
lot more were asked, less politely, in quarters close to the
Khedive.

The Minister issued a further statement saying that his
decision was irrevocable and then prudently left for the
country.

It was rumoured that he was in deep mourning for a
relative who had recently died in some obscure village in
the extreme south and even further west of the country,
close to the borders with—? No one was exactly sure but
it was exceedingly hot there and scorpions abounded and
no one proposed going there to find out.

Mr Aziz, left to field questions, learned a new meaning
for the expression 'field trials'. He had, however, taken
the precaution of sending the seed samples abroad before
agreeing to answer any questions and after a day or two
the barrage died down.

Not so in the case of Owen, whose part in the affair
only gradually came to light. The business community was
outraged and asked whose side the Mamur Zapt Johnny
was on. Comments were made in the Club which were
intended to be overheard. Even Paul was put out.

'We've got enough people meddling as it is,' he complained, 'me, for one. We don't want any more people

muddying the pitch, or whatever these strange men do when they get on the sportsfield. You should have told me first.'

'I thought you might prefer not to know.'

'Who do you think I am,' asked Paul tartly, 'a Minister? Someone's got to have a grip on things.'

'That, actually, was the question I wanted to ask you,' said Owen. 'Who is the person in the Ministries who has a grip on this deal between the Agricultural Bank and the Ministry of Agriculture?'

'Well—'

'Who is actually going to sign the damned thing?'

'Some poor sap. Signing, however, is nothing to do with it. The answer to your question is Abdul Mursa.'

Owen recognized the name of someone high up at the Ministry of Finance.

'Why?' asked Paul.

'I think I'd better see him.'

'I think you'd better not,' said Paul, 'not for quite some time.'

'You see, if he's steering it—'

'What is "it"?'

'This dubious deal and the dubious goings-on around it.'

'I'm not sure the deal *is* dubious,' said Paul 'About the goings-on, however . . .'

'You're the one who told me to investigate them.'

'Osman Fingari?' Paul frowned. '*Something's* going on, certainly. But I'd be surprised if Abdul Mursa was in on it. He's an honest man. As they go, of course.'

'He might be doing someone a favour.'

'Ah, that,' said Paul, 'is quite possible. Anyone who gets as high as he has done might well have a lot of favours to pay back.'

'Have you any idea who he might be paying them to?'

'I could give you a list.'

'Please do. Would the list include Pashas? Ali Reza Pasha, for instance?'

'It might. But, look, if I do this for you, will you do something for me?'

'We are all in the business of favours,' said Owen.

'Thank you. Well, the favour I want you to do me is not to cause any more trouble for a day or two. I've quite enough as it is. Go and play with Zeinab.'

If Owen was extremely unpopular in some circles, however, he was suddenly unexpectedly popular in others.

Mr Sidki rushed round to congratulate him.

'I never knew the Minister had it in him!' he declared. 'It appears he has, and if so someone must have put it there. A triumph! For you, for us and for the fellahin.'

Owen was not so sure. He had talked to Yussuf that morning. The orderly had come in unusually depressed. He had, it appeared, been negotiating a loan with the Agricultural Bank. Negotiations had suddenly been suspended.

'But, Yussuf, you don't *need* a loan. You already have loans up to your eyeballs.'

'Yes, I do, effendi,' wailed Yussuf. 'How else am I to pay for seed?'

Owen had heard this before.

'I suppose I could make you an advance,' he said grudgingly.

'No, no, effendi, this really is for seed.'

'Three pounds, then.'

'Alas, effendi,' said Yussuf sadly, 'I need fifty.'

So Owen wasn't sure about it being a triumph as far as the fellahin were concerned. Paul had told him that if the Agricultural Bank was unable to raise a loan it might well collapse. Then what would the fellahin do? Go back to the traditional moneylender at 75%?

'The Government should make a loan,' said Mr Sidki.

'The Government *needs* a loan,' said Paul. 'Otherwise it will go under, too.'

In his jubilation Mr Sidki was disposed to forget that what had originally sparked things off was Osman Fingari's suicide.

'I still can't see what brought it about,' said Owen.

'Pressure,' said Mr Sidki, 'pressure.'

'Who from?'

'The Bank, of course. To get the deal completed. Oh, you won't believe the pressure they put him under. Especially when they began to realize he was dragging his feet.'

'Dragging his feet?'

Mr Sidki stared at him.

'Of course! He was opposed to the whole thing, you know.'

'I didn't know.'

'But of course! He was one of us.'

'One of us?'

'A sympathizer. Politically. From the time when he was in college. We have a lot of support among students, Captain Owen, we do some of our best recruiting there. And then afterwards we kept in touch, especially when he went to the Ministry.'

'Public Works?'

'Yes. But then when he told us he was moving to Agriculture, well, we were delighted. We had some inkling that a deal was in the offing but lacked precise information. So when we heard he was going to Agriculture we thought he might be in a position to supply it. And then, when we found out he was actually handling the deal, we thought this is our chance.'

'To do what, Mr Sidki?'

'To delay the deal. You see, we thought that if we had longer we might be able to rouse public opinion against it, might even be able to stop it altogether. We instructed Osman to play for time. But then, I think, they began to suspect.'

'And put pressure on him?'

'Yes.'

'And you think this was what led Mr Fingari to commit suicide?'

'Yes.'

'Mr Sidki, when we spoke before, you used a word which implied something more than pressure.'

'Did I?'

'You spoke of him as being killed.'

Mr Sidki hesitated.

'Does it not amount to the same thing?'

'I don't think it does.'

Mr Sidki hesitated again, then took Owen confidentially by the arm.

'Isn't it a question of the degree and nature of the pressure?' He bent his head close to Owen's. 'You see, Captain Owen, we suspect that there was something which gave them a hold over him and that when they began to suspect, they, well . . .'

'Used this knowledge?'

'Threatened to use it, perhaps.'

'Blackmail?'

Sidki bent his head even closer.

'That is what we suspect.'

'You don't think, Mr Sidki, that you yourselves may have been to blame? You, too, were exerting pressure. Perhaps between the pressures . . .'

Mr Sidki released his arm and stepped back, horrified.

'Certainly not, Captain Owen! Certainly not!'

Ali was waiting for him as he came down the steps of the Bab-el-Khalk.

'Effendi!' he hissed. 'I have important news.'

Owen felt in his pocket.

'What is it?' he said.

'You have a rival.'

'Rival?' said Owen, bewildered.

'She is seeing another.'

'Aisha?'

'Just so, effendi,' said Ali, looking wise. 'Appetite will out. I must say, it comes as a bit of a surprise in Aisha's case, but these quiet ones—'

'All right, all right. Who is this man?'

'Someone from the past.'

'Is his name Jabir?'

Ali looked surprised. 'No, effendi. His name is Selim.'

'Oh, Selim. I know about that.'

Ali fell in alongside him as Owen turned under the trees.

'The question is, effendi, what we are going to do. I am willing to help but, well,' Ali admitted, 'my experience is limited.'

'A good job, too.'

'We could try poison. You would have to get it, though, as Abdul Mali refused to sell it me now.'

'Now?' said Owen, halting.

'Since the business of the sheep.'

'What business of the sheep?' said Owen severely.

'Mohammed Siftaq's sheep. Well, he had no cause to be rude, did he? The harem window was open, what did he expect? She did it deliberately, I'm sure.'

'Ali—'

'Anyway, it wasn't poison the sheep died of. It sicked it all up. No, it choked itself on some very gristly offal it found in the street. Effendi?'

'Yes?'

'Is there any way in which we could get him to choke himself?'

'It hasn't come to that, Ali. However, since you are here, can you arrange another meeting with Aisha for me?'

Ali, surprisingly, was silent.

'Well?'

'Effendi,' said Ali reluctantly. 'I could, but—'

'Well?'

'Effendi, Aisha has been good to me. She is a good girl. Her appetite is obviously beginning to get out of hand, but all the same—'

'Shut up, Ali,' said Owen.

They walked a little way in silence. Owen's hand was still in his pocket, a fact which Ali had been contemplating.

'Effendi,' he said at last, 'I will do it. But you must promise me you will not kill her. Beat, yes, but—'

'I have no intention of even touching her. I just want to see her.'

'Well, of course, effendi. Passion—'

They met in an alleyway behind an oil press. Owen recognized that it was difficult to find a pretext for women to go out, never mind meet anybody and paid inner tribute to Ali's ingenuity. Nevertheless, as he crouched among the sacks of sesame seed, barely able to breathe because of the heavy, sweet, sickly smell of the pressed oil which hung over everything, he felt uneasily that Ali's talents were beginning to run away with him.

The dark veiled form of a woman with a huge jar on her head came into the alleyway and hovered uncertainly.

'Aisha?'

Reassured, the figure advanced. Beside the wall there was a pile of barrels. One of them was raised on stones and already spigoted. Aisha set her jar down in front of it and turned the spigot. Oil began to flow steadily.

'Effendi?'

'I have a few questions. Can you help me again?'

'I will try.'

'Good. Then, first, can you tell me if Osman was interested in politics?'

'He was as all the young men are, effendi.'

'Did he talk about it?'

'Oh, yes. Sometimes he was angry.'

'What was he angry about?'

'The fellahin. The British.'

'The British, I can understand. Why was he angry about the fellahin?'

'He said things were bad for them. That this was a bad time. That is why he was glad when he moved to the new Ministry. He thought he might be able to do them good.'

'How?'

'I do not know, effendi. Through his work, perhaps.'

'Did he go to meetings?'

'I do not think so, effendi. That is—' she hesitated— 'after I spoke to him.'

'Why did you speak to him, Aisha?'

'It was just after he had joined the Ministry, the first one. There was a demonstration. He told me about it afterwards. People had thrown stones. I was angry. I said, "If you do that, you will soon lose your job. Then where will you be?" And I think he listened to me, for after that there was no more.'

'Was this about the time that he met up again with Jabir?'

Aisha thought.

'It was about that time, yes, effendi. But I do not think that it was anything to do with Jabir.'

'No, no. I was thinking that perhaps Jabir turned his mind away from that sort of thing and towards other things.'

'If he did,' said Aisha bitterly, 'it was the first good he has done him.'

She turned off the flow of oil but still crouched by the jar as if she was watching it fill.

'My other question is about Jabir. Can you speak of him?'

'If I must,' said Aisha in a low voice.

'It relates to the last few weeks. You have already told me that in that time Osman became a changed man.'

'Yes.'

'Things weighed on his mind, but not in an ordinary way. Much, much more heavily.'

'Yes, effendi.'

'And in that time, was he seeing Jabir?'

'Yes, effendi.'

Aisha's voice was almost inaudible.

'Are you sure, Aisha? How do you know? You said he did not speak to you.'

There was a long silence, so long that he was beginning to think she might not have heard.

'He came to me,' she said at last.

'Osman?'

'No, no.' She made a gesture with her hand. 'Jabir.'

'Jabir came to you?'

'Yes. He wanted to speak with me. He said Osman had given permission. I knew he wanted to ask me and—and I would not let him. I would not even let him come in. I turned him from the door.'

'What did he say to you?'

'Just what I have said. That Osman had given him permission. I would not let him say any more. It—it was nothing, effendi. But that is how I know Osman had been seeing him.'

'And you do not know what they spoke of?'

'Only this, effendi. Only this.'

She gave a little sob.

'I shall not keep you further, Aisha,' said Owen gently. 'It is just that I am trying very hard to find something that Osman may have done which gave others a hold over him.'

'He had done something wrong, effendi,' said Aisha, sobbing. 'I know he had.'

'And you have no idea what? Did he ever mention the name Tufa to you?'

Aisha shook her head. 'No, effendi,' she said.

Owen waited for a few moments after Aisha had gone

before climbing out from behind his sacks. Ali was waiting for him at the end of the alleyway.

'Effendi!' he said agitatedly. 'He is here!'

'Who?'

'Your rival. Shall we strike now, effendi? God has delivered him into our hands.'

'Well—'

'I will lure him up a dark street and then you . . . I think it is best if you do it, effendi, for he is bigger than I.'

'No, Ali.'

'No?' said Ali, disappointed. 'Not yet? Well, of course, it is for you to decide but such golden opportunities do not grow on trees. Still,' he said, cheering up, 'they do say that revenge is a dish best eaten cold.'

'Thank you, Ali. Now can you tell me where Selim is?'

'You wish to measure him? This way, effendi.'

The barber was in full spate as they arrived. A small crowd had gathered round him and at the back of the crowd was Selim.

'The man is right!' he was declaring, with a great wave of his scissors. The customer in the chair flinched and looked miserable. From the rear of the small crowd Selim nodded approvingly.

'We must stand up for ourselves! We must get up off our backsides!'

'I would willingly get off mine,' said the customer in the chair, 'if only you'd stop talking and get on with it.'

The barber ignored him.

'The man's right!' he said excitedly. 'We've got to do something. Otherwise it will be too late. First the *kuttub*. Then the hospital. Then the mosque. Then the House for the Aged. What'll it be next, I wonder? The graveyard? Yes! Even in the graveyard our bones cannot lie in peace!'

'What's the graveyard got to do with it?' asked someone.

'Haven't you heard? They're driving a road right smack through the middle of it,' replied his neighbour.

'Excuse me—' began Selim, a little anxiously.

'And now it's the water!' cried the barber.

'Water?' said Selim, taken aback.

'Yes. Close the *kuttub* first, then the fountains below. That's what they'll do. You mark my words!' said the barber with an extravagant flourish.

'Oi!' cried the customer in alarm, as the blades went past him.

'Take our water from us,' cried the barber, 'and you take our lives!'

'There are other pumps besides those at the fountain-house,' someone objected.

The crowd, however, was caught up in the sweep of the barber's rhetoric.

'The bastards! They're after our water now!'

'They'll have us by the throat!' shouted the barber, clutching at his and gasping dramatically. 'Take our water and there'll be nothing left for us to do but die!'

'I shall die first,' said the customer sitting in the chair, 'only it'll be from old age, waiting for you to finish trimming my beard!'

The barber turned back to him in a fury.

Selim was mopping his brow when Owen came up to him.

'It doesn't seem to be quite as straightforward as I thought,' he said.

'But why me?' said Owen.

Zokosis smiled.

'I think, Captain Owen, that if you were frank you would admit that you view me with a certain amount of suspicion. It is precisely for that reason.'

The Chairman of the Khedivial Agricultural Society looked puzzled.

'The Society has built its reputation on employing the best people,' he said. 'Pay the most, get the best.'

'I am afraid I am committed to my public duties.'

'This would be in your free time.'

'Even so—'

'I don't think it's incompatible with your public duties,' said Zokosis. 'Indeed, rather the reverse.'

'You see, Owen,' said the Chairman, 'because of all the furore there's been about this—quite a lot of which, frankly, has been of your making—the Society's got to be seen to be above board. Well, we *are* above board and we'll damned well show it by using you. That way there'll be no doubt.'

'This is of more than usual importance, Captain Owen,' said Zokosis, 'or we wouldn't waste your time. The deal has run into difficulties, I don't mind admitting it. The people who are going to finance it want cast-iron assurances. The reports on these tests are crucial to our success. And it's not just the Bank that will go under if we fail, but thousands of fellahin.'

'You owe it to us,' said the Chairman determinedly. 'You're the one who's raised doubts. We've tried to answer them honestly. All we want from you is help in making sure that nothing goes wrong at this end.'

'Surely, anyone could meet Monsieur Paparemborde?'

'We could send an orderly down. But if we did and if the report was favourable to our case, people would say— *you* would probably say—that we had rigged it. We want *you* to be in charge and then there can be no doubt.'

'This is hardly a part of my duties—'

'Quite so,' put in Zokosis, 'and that is why we are asking you to go in your free time and are prepared to pay you. We'll make it worth your while, of course, but there'll be nothing under-the-counter about it. The charge will be in the Society's published accounts.'

'Published?' asked Owen.

'Accounts,' said the Chairman hastily.

It seemed unreasonable to refuse. He stipulated that the report should be opened in his presence so that there would be no tampering with it *after* it had been received by the Society and was reassured that they made no objection.

'Glad you're willing to help us,' said the Chairman, shaking hands. 'As I say, we're not paying much—'

Zokosis touched him on the sleeve.

'Oh yes. When we discussed this at our Committee, several of my colleagues wondered if the task could be combined with another project we have in mind. Or rather, they have in mind. It's a group of our members who are exploring the possibility of developing a courier service between Alexandria and Cairo. They wondered if while you were undertaking this mission you could think about it as a prototype and perhaps make a report—'

'I hardly think I'm qualified—'

'On the security aspects,' Zokosis put in quickly.

'I'll think about it.'

The boat arrived on Friday, which was the Moslem sabbath, so Owen was free to go down to Alexandria and meet the Frenchman. He was on his way to India but had been entrusted by his colleagues at the Institute with their analysis of the tests.

This was not the analysis that Mr Aziz had requested but a separate one asked for by the Society.

'The Institute's the leading one in the field,' the Chairman had said. 'Let's not mess around; let's go straight to the top.'

Monsieur Paparemborde handed the envelope over to Owen, he caught the next train to Cairo and the following morning delivered the package to the Society's offices.

Hiscock, the Society's Scientific Consultant, opened the envelope.

'Disappointing in one respect,' he said, reading the report; 'they say they can comment only on our own testing. In order to be able to confirm our findings they will need to replicate the study independently, which will take some time. However,' he looked triumphantly at Owen, 'they have only minor reservations, minor, indeed, about our methodology.'

'Glad to hear it,' said Owen.

'Send you a cheque, old man,' said the Chairman.

It arrived on Owen's desk the next day and was for the agreed sum. He pocketed it with pleasure. It would about do to buy a bottle of champagne for himself and Zeinab at the opera that evening.

Later in the morning another cheque arrived. It was from the people who had commissioned a report from him on their projected courier service. It was for a very considerable sum, which was all the more surprising as he had not yet had time to write his report.

'Very nice!' said Zeinab that evening. 'Let's have another one!'

As they drank it, he told her about the second cheque.

'It's nice to know your talents are appreciated,' she said.

'I haven't had a chance to show any talent yet,' he objected.

'If I know Cairo,' said Zeinab, smiling, 'you soon will have.'

The Widow Shawquat, taking the view that men, if left to their own devices, could not be trusted to get it right, accompanied them to the House of the Mufti. She did not go in with them, however, but sat herself down in the road outside the gate.

'Now have you got it straight?' she said. 'Remember what I told you. (And see he doesn't go on too long,' she muttered aside to Owen.)

'Of course I've got it straight, woman,' said the Sheikh testily.

He grasped his stick and strode on ahead through the gates.

The Widow watched him with affection.

'Dear Man!' she said. 'His soul is in Heaven. Unfortunately, his mind is sometimes there, too.'

Owen followed the Sheikh in. The Sheikh had insisted on being responsible for arrangements. Owen had taken the precaution, however, of phoning beforehand to see whether they were expected. They weren't.

The young man in the outer office consulted his list.

'The Mufti? Today? I'm afraid not.'

'But I phoned,' protested Owen.

'I sent Abu,' protested the Sheikh.

'I'm sorry,' said the young man.

The Sheikh drew himself up to his full, rickety height.

'Tell His Dear Self that it is I, Hussein Al-Jamal Abd-el-Assid who stands at his door!' he said.

'Look—' began the young man.

The Sheikh took a step forward and banged his stick on the top of the desk.

'Aside!' he shouted. 'Aside! Do we stop just because the thorns are in our way? Hesitate, when they seek to bar the road? Let me tell you this, O foolish boy, the road I travel on is never barred. It is a pilgrimage of grace—'

The door at the end of the room opened and a burly man in robe and turban came through.

'Is that not the voice of my old friend, Hussein Al-Jamal Abd-el-Assid?' he asked.

The Sheikh stumbled forward.

'And they would keep me from you!' he cried.

'Well, well, well,' said the Mufti. 'You wanted to see me? Then come inside.'

'But it's not in the Appointments List!' protested the young man.

'It should be,' said Owen. 'I phoned to let you know we were coming.'

'You are together?' said the Mufti, looking puzzled. He shrugged his shoulders. 'Very well, then.'

After the greetings, which were prolonged, and the

inquiries after health, which seemed unusually genuine, the Mufti asked their business.

'Let him tell you,' said the Sheikh gruffly, with a nod of his head in Owen's direction. 'He stands more chance of getting it right.'

Owen explained about the *waqfs*. The Mufti listened with great attention.

'A road through the Derb Aiah? But where would it go to?'

Owen had intended to keep quiet about the larger north–south road on the grounds that if the Mufti so far hadn't heard of it, so much the better, but he found himself forced to add that bit of information, too.

The Mufti's eyes widened.

'But that is lunacy!' he cried.

Owen nodded.

'That is what I think, too.'

'It is insane even to think of it!' He began to walk up and down the room in perturbed fashion. 'Madness!' he kept saying to himself. 'Madness!'

The Sheikh watched him for some time.

'Well, Ali,' he said at last. 'What are we going to do?'

The Mufti pulled himself together and came back to them.

'I'll appeal against the *waqfs*,' he said. 'That's for a start. Ordinarily I wouldn't do a thing like that, I leave it to the Ministry. It's a question of law and I don't normally like to interfere. But I'll certainly do it this time. But that's not enough, is it? We've got to stop the roads altogether. Now, young man, who did you say you were? The Mamur Zapt? The Mamur Zapt! Well, surely you can do something?'

'Not really,' said Owen. 'At least, not easily. I don't really have the power.'

The Mufti looked surprised.

'I thought the British had *all* the power,' he said.

'Not power,' said Owen, 'influence, perhaps.'

'Well, can't you use your influence?'

'I don't have enough,' said Owen. 'I was hoping you could see your way to using yours.'

'Oh, I don't have any influence,' said the Mufti. 'No one listens to me. Unless I threaten to start a war. And I don't really want to do that. At least, not over this.'

'Old, young,' said the Sheikh. 'Foxes, both of you. Why don't you put your heads together and avert the Camel of Destruction?'

The phone was ringing as Owen entered his office. It was Paul.

'The people who were going to finance the deal with the Agricultural Bank have pulled out,' he said. 'Zokosis has been here. The Minister of Finance has been here. The chairmen of all the banks have been here. Even the Khedive wants to see the Consul-General. We're in trouble. You,' said Paul with emphasis, 'are in trouble.'

CHAPTER 12

Owen called for Zeinab in a two-horse barouche. This had never happened before and Zeinab was impressed. Usually, he collected her in an ordinary, moth-eaten street arabeah.

Tonight, admittedly, was a special occasion. They were to see a performance of *Aïda*, the great opera originally commissioned from Verdi by the Khedive to celebrate the opening of the Suez Canal. The opera, though extremely popular in Cairo because of its Egyptian theme, was rarely performed because of the huge cost of staging it and neither Owen nor Zeinab had seen it before.

The Opera House itself had been built to commemorate the same event and on a corresponding scale and its huge cost, it was commonly asserted, had been the thing which had finally tipped the scales in the Khedive's bankruptcy and led to the intervention of the Western powers.

But for the Opera House, Owen explained to Zeinab, the British would not have been there. Zeinab replied that, immoderately as she loved opera, and prepared though she was to make personal exceptions, the price did not seem worth paying.

A particular privilege with respect to opera went with the post of Mamur Zapt. It was the possession of a regular box at the Opera House. Owen, when he had first taken up the post, had seen it as a particularly imaginative way of encouraging the arts.

So it was, but not quite in the way he thought. Determined that the House should be a success, the Khedive instructed all his nobles to attend it; and he had sent the Mamur Zapt there to make sure that they did.

This was no longer one of Owen's duties but he still retained the perquisite. Without it, Zeinab assured him, he would be nothing in her eyes.

In view of the exceptional nature of the occasion, Zeinab had attired herself exceptionally and was sparkling all over. Most of the other ladies present, it turned out, had made the same decision and although the general lustre was dimmed when they retired behind the harem grills with which the boxes were surrounded, at the Interval it shone forth in all its splendour.

Owen normally took Zeinab down to the Saloon. This evening, though, he had dinner served in their box. Suffragis in splendid white gowns, turbans and red sashes pushed in a small table and proceeded to serve the dishes. Champagne in a bucket stood handily by.

Zeinab accepted all this as her due. Even she, however, was mildly surprised when yet more goodies and yet more champagne appeared at the second Interval.

'Are you sure it's all right?' she said, a little anxiously.

Owen sipped the champagne.

'Oh yes. I think so. A little over-chilled, perhaps. I don't care what anyone says, I think you *can* over-ice champagne.'

'That was not what I meant,' said Zeinab, putting her hand on his. 'Aren't you overdoing it a little?'

'No, I don't think so,' said Owen.

'Because if you're doing it for me—'

> ' "For lady, you deserve this state;
> Nor would I love at lower rate," '

said Owen.

'Well,' said Zeinab, melting, 'put like that . . .'

Opera started late in Cairo and continued long, and *Aïda* continued longer than most. In the third Interval, in the small hours, cognac came with the coffee and Zeinab felt moved to protest.

'Are you sure you can afford it, darling?'

'Oh yes.'

But Zeinab was not put off.

'Where,' she demanded, 'is the money coming from?'

Owen raised his glass.

'Let us drink,' he said, 'to those excellent people who provide me with my salary.'

Zeinab, uncertainly and unconvinced, raised her glass.

'A Mr Sabry would like to make your acquaintance,' said Nikos, 'a Mr *Jabir* Sabry.'

'Would he now?' said Owen.

'Drinks before lunch. At Shepheard's.'

Jabir was no longer quite as young or quite as slim as he had been. His suit, that of the standard young effendi, was modish but in the fashion of a few years before and his body strained against it. He wore a dark glasses even indoors. He ordered whiskies for them both and then led Owen over to a corner where they would not be disturbed.

'It is a pleasure to meet you, Captain Owen,' he said as

they sat down. 'We are so glad you have been able to help us. I read your report with great interest and can assure you that it will have a considerable influence on our thinking. There are just one or two points I would like to take up with you if I may.'

Jabir had certainly done his homework. His questions were acute and probed at detail.

'I would have thought it was not so much the detail, though, as the principle,' said Owen. 'I am surprised that you are thinking in terms of a courier service just when so many new forms of communication are becoming available. The development of the sea-bed cable—'

'It's certainly speeded things up. We get an answer from the Paris Bourse the same day. But speed is not the only consideration. Confidentiality, indeed secrecy, is sometimes important, especially in banking And when legal matters are involved you have to deal with the actual documents. There's no getting away from couriers.'

'You work for a bank?'

'Sometimes. In this instance, though, I am representing a group of people who think they can exploit the needs of the banking system. It's developing very rapidly, you know, not just here but throughout the Middle East.'

'The courier service would specialize in bank work?'

'Initially, yes, though any work, really, that requires confidentiality. And that, of course, is why we are so glad that you have been able to help us. The security aspect must be paramount. And who better to advise us on that than the Mamur Zapt?'

'Glad to help,' said Owen.

'We're hoping you would consider helping us on a permanent basis.'

'I am afraid I am rather committed to my present duties.'

'Oh, there's no conflict. We are only talking about advice from time to time. For which, of course, we would be prepared to pay.'

He mentioned a sum.

'That is considerable,' said Owen.

'We suspect that if the courier service is successful, other groups will soon be wanting to start one. And we'd like to make sure that you are already committed. We were thinking of this as an annual retainer.'

'It's even more considerable, then.'

Jabir laughed. 'It's what you're worth, Captain Owen, and what you would be worth to us.'

'It's nice of you to say so. I shall certainly think your offer over very seriously.'

'Excellent! Let us drink to that.'

He ordered two more whiskies.

'There is just one thing, though, that we ought to clear up,' said Owen.

'Yes?'

'Who exactly is it that you are representing? Who would I be working for?'

Jabir laughed again. 'No secret about that,' he said. 'At least, not as far as you are concerned, Captain Owen. Though I wouldn't like it broadcast too widely until we're a little further on.'

He mentioned a few names. That of Ali Reza Pasha was among them.

'All very respectable men,' he said. 'Does that set your mind at rest?'

'It does indeed,' said Owen.

The drinks arrived. They raised their glasses.

'I believe you knew an acquaintance of mine,' said Owen, as he put his glass down.

'Really?'

'Osman Fingari.'

Jabir looked down at the table and sighed.

'Poor Osman!'

'You were a particular friend of his?'

'I wouldn't say that. We were at school together and

then we didn't see each other for a year or two. But then
we met up again recently.'

'When he joined the Ministry?'

'Yes. You say he was a friend of yours, Captain Owen?'

'Hardly a friend. A passing acquaintance.'

'You are investigating his death?'

'Oh no. The Parquet does that. If it is required, that is.
My interest is rather more general. The authorities are a
little concerned. Not very concerned, but a little. When
someone commits suicide, you know, questions get asked.
Was he overworked? Is the Department understaffed? Or
poorly managed?'

'Osman was certainly hard-working. I remember thinking several times that perhaps he was overdoing it.'

'Really?'

'Oh yes.' Jabir hesitated. 'There were other signs, too.
The occasional drink. Incidentally . . . ?'

'Thank you.'

A waiter brought two more glasses.

'No doubt the situation contributed,' said Owen.

'The situation?'

'I gather there's something of a banking crisis '

'Yes, indeed. But . . . Osman was in the Department of
Agriculture, was he not?'

'Oh, come, Mr Sabry!' Owen said, smiling, 'I'm sure
you know as well as I do, with your banking connections,
about the business with the Agricultural Bank?'

'Well!' Jabir laughed. 'Perhaps I do.'

'Additional work, difficult circumstances. I'm sure that
can't have helped. Wouldn't you agree?'

'Oh yes, indeed.'

'You saw him just before it happened, didn't you? Would
you say he was under strain?'

'Oh, very much so.'

'Any *particular* cause of strain, do you know?'

Jabir hesitated. 'Just general pressure.'

'To conclude the deal? Was there a time limit?'

'Oh yes.'

'That might have been it, then, mightn't it? He was worried about completing it on time. The only thing is—'

'Yes?'

'Several people have suggested to me that in fact he was not hurrying. Deliberately not hurrying.'

'Deliberately?'

'Was that, I wonder, the impression of your colleagues, Mr Sabry? Your banking colleagues, that is?'

Jabir hesitated.

'Yes,' he said slowly. 'I believe it was.'

'And why was that, do you think?'

'I've no idea.'

'Someone pressing the other way, perhaps?'

Jabir shot a glance at him.

'Why would anyone be doing that?'

'Because they were rivals, perhaps? You spoke of rivals earlier.'

'Ah, but that was quite different. There are no rivals here,' said Jabir positively.

'Well, perhaps not rivals. Opponents, let's say. Political opponents?'

There was a little silence.

'You could be right,' said Jabir.

'Because if I was, and there were people applying pressure from several directions, and because of one of the pressures Osman was, let's say, dragging his feet, then those applying pressure from the opposite direction might feel they needed to exert something extra in the way of pressure.'

'How would they do that?' muttered Jabir.

'You tell me,' said Owen.

'And did he?' asked Georgiades.

'What do you think?'

'I think he didn't buy you any more drinks after that.'

'Correct.'

'But the answer is in any case obvious,' said Georgiades: 'Tufa.'

'Yes,' said Owen. 'That's right. I was puzzled at first that Ali Reza and the Trans-Levant were in on the act. It seemed too small. If they were just interested in the money, that is. But if they were interested in something else . . .'

'Like the deal with the Agricultural Bank.'

'Yes. And, having got their man into place, wanted to be sure that he would do as he was told . . .'

'Tufa was just right. They involved him at the beginning when they got him to approve the first application. And then they involved him again when they applied to register the change of land use. His initials on both. So they had got him. If they ever needed to get him.'

'I think they did need to get him. Or threaten to get him. When it became clear that he was dragging his feet.'

'Who is "they"?' asked Georgiades.

'Ali Reza, of course. He was the man with influence at the Ministry. He was the one who was able to get Fingari transferred and put in the right place. But I suspect he may have been just a helper. There were others involved.'

'The Trans-Levant Bank, for instance.'

'Yes. Jabir could have been a go-between in both directions. Not just Ali Reza's man at the Bank, but, more to the point, the Bank's way of approaching Ali Reza.'

'You think the initiative came from the Bank?'

'We're talking about a banking deal. And we're talking about something big, big even for Ali Reza.'

'How big is the Trans-Levant?'

'That's what I'm wondering. Get Nikos to have a look. He's done something on that shell company, hasn't he? He may already have an idea. But get him to check on some of the other things they're involved in. Especially—' Owen stopped.

'Especially?'

'Tufa was a land deal, wasn't it? Get him to look at other land deals. And in particular—'

'Yes?'

'Ones around the Bab-el-Azab.'

It was only gradually that Owen's part in the Minister's decision to send seed abroad for independent testing became known. Owen suspected that the Khedivial Agricultural Society had not known about it when they had asked him to undertake the journey to Alexandria for them. He thought it likely that they would not be asking him again.

Among the Nationalists, though, his name was murmured with relish, and some surprise. He even found himself mentioned favourably in some of the most radical Nationalist newspapers.

He was not foolish enough to imagine that this would continue for long; nor did it.

Opening a copy of *Al-Lewa* one morning, he found himself the subject of the leading article. It described his visit to Alexandria on behalf of the Khedivial Agricultural Society and was sufficiently well-informed as to refer to a separate commission from 'a notorious ring of Pashas'.

The article was long on implication and short on detail but it did print the exact size of the sum that Owen had received and made much of the discrepancy between it and the nature of the services allegedly rendered.

Was not this, the article inquired, yet another instance of the corruption in which the country's Government was steeped? Yet one more illustration of the dubious links between business, Administration and, yes, the Khedive, for whom, it was implied, the Khedivial Agricultural Society was but a front? One more betrayal of decent fellahin by those responsible for the direction of the country?

It was particularly sad to find the Mamur Zapt so

directly implicated. There had recently been indications that he was taking a more liberal line. Alas, this was probably merely another illustration of the subterfuge for which the Mamur Zapt was famous.

Corruption, the article concluded, was all around. The only answer was to get rid of the lot of them: Khedive, Pashas, Government, British, bankers, moneylenders, barbers—

Barbers? Owen summoned Yussuf. Why barbers?

Yussuf shuffled his feet.

'In our village,' he said finally, 'it is Abdul the barber who arranges the loans.'

'But surely he has no money to lend?'

'No, but Ibrahim has and Abdul acts for him.'

'Why does not Ibrahim act for himself?'

'Because he lives in another village, effendi.'

At last Owen understood. In the small villages of the Egyptian countryside the barber was often a leading figure. Where there was no *omda*, or headman, he sometimes acted as the local registrar.

Of an evening the men of the village would gather round to admire the barber's art and join in the conversation. This left the barber handily placed for the discharge of commissions, especially on behalf of those outside the village.

Agent for the local moneylender and representative of the Government! No wonder the rural barber was added to the Nationalists' hate list.

The town barber was, of course, quite different. He was often radical, as in the case of Owen's friend in the Derb Aiah, and very popular with the Nationalists.

'Yussuf,' said Owen sternly, 'you must not go to Ibrahim. He will charge you a fifty per cent rate of interest.'

'More,' said Yussuf sadly. 'Abdul told me yesterday it would be seventy-five per cent if I did not go to him soon.'

'You steer clear of him,' Owen advised.

Yussuf spread his hands.

'How can I, effendi? I must buy seed. And now that the Bank has refused . . .'

Owen sat considering the nation's finances for some time, an activity to which he was not much accustomed. They seemed more complicated than he had thought. Banks, he was against, and moneylenders, too. Large landowners he was not greatly in favour of, rich pashas in general even less. The business community did not fill him with enthusiasm.

But abolish all these—and he was astonished to find the similarity between his own thinking and that of the Nationalists—and where was the money to come from?

The phone rang.

'Gareth,' said Paul sternly, 'is this true?'

'Is what true?'

'About the money.'

He quoted the relevant part of *Al-Lewa*.

'Certainly,' said Owen.

There was a long silence.

'I'm sorry,' said Paul.

All Cairo loved a procession, which was just as well for there were plenty of them. There were wedding processions and funeral processions; there were processions to mark the end of Ramadan and the Rising of the Waters; there was a procession to 'smell the air', when half of Cairo trooped out of the city on the first day of the *khamsin* to savour the coming of spring.

There were processions to mark saints' days and there was certainly at least one saint's day every week. There was a procession to mark the Birthday of the Prophet, marred only by the fact that the interfering British would no longer allow devotees to lie on their faces in the street for the Descendant of the Prophet to ride over. Similar interference, it was rumoured, was projected for the night of the Ashura, when the devout marched through the streets slashing themselves with swords and knives.

The best time for processions was during the pilgrim season. Almost every day private pilgrims returning from Mecca were escorted back to their houses by processions sometimes half a mile in length. When the bulk parties of pilgrims arrived, by train now, the procession jammed the city for days. The climax was the Return of the Carpet from Mecca—an occasion which Owen had good cause to remember.

Processions did not consist simply of people marching. They included palanquins and bands and acrobats and masqueraders. They included people doing comic turns — usually of a scurrilous nature—in cages carried on marchers' shoulders. They included people dancing and people carrying their restaurants around with them and giant floats with papier-mâché figures. All the fun of the fair, you might say; only a moving fair.

The British, when they came, had no idea how to police this lot. That policing was needed was self-evident. Big numbers in confined places; people enjoying themselves. That spelt trouble.

They tried lining the streets with constables. It did not work because the constables were simply lads from the country and either watched jaw-dropped and spellbound or else joined in.

After a while the authorities realized that the occasions needed little special policing except when they were on an unusually large scale. They confined their efforts to political demonstrations, of which, with the growth of Nationalism, there was an increasing number.

These certainly did need policing, not so much because of the threat these posed to the authorities, although that was not how they saw it, but because they tended to spill over into violence directed at some minority group or other.

So when the Mufti proposed his Grand March, Owen's

first question was about the nature of the procession.

'Political, certainly,' said the Mufti. 'We want to influence the Prime Minister, don't we?'

Owen explained his difficulty.

'It's hardly religious,' said the Mufti. 'I could say it was to stop mosques being knocked down but then that very definitely *would* lead to trouble.'

'I was wondering,' said Owen diffidently, 'whether the point could be made implicitly in some way. You know, the procession could ostensibly be about something else, to celebrate a saint or something, but somehow make the point— ?'

'We could certainly celebrate a saint,' said the Mufti, thinking. 'There are several to choose from. There is no need to be too pedantic about actual day of birth. How about Sheikh Abd Al-Samad?'

'He seems as good as any other.'

'Better,' said the Mufti, 'because what he is noted for is averting the Camel of Destruction.'

'How did he do that?'

'He lay down in its path. The Camel swerved when it saw the Sheikh and the town was saved.'

'He will do very nicely,' said Owen.

The date and route of the March was announced. The procession would start outside the Mosque of Ibu Tulun, proceed westward past the Mosque of Sayida Zeinab (Owen liked this), march northwards through the Ministerial Quarter (unusual, this, for a saint's procession) to the Bab-el-Luk, swing eastwards past the Khedive's Palace (so that the Khedive could share their delight) and the Police Headquarters at the Bab-el Khalk (where the police could keep an eye on them) and finally march east out of the city towards the Mokattam Hills, where a *fantasia* would be waiting for them.

This was important both because it was a great draw

and because it was out of town, so here would be a fair chance of everything ending peaceably.

A *fantasia* was, basically, fun and games. A space would be made ready with lots of little booths made out of carpet in which sights might be seen (like the Woman With Two Heads) and entertainment experienced (like the Juggling Snake). There would be a variety of food stalls so that the procession could refresh itself on cakes (but not ale), sweetmeats, nuts, roasts and tea.

After which they would all, so Owen hoped, go peaceably to bed.

McPhee, the Deputy Commandant of the Cairo Police, would look after this end. He had a collector's interest in saints' days: although he was a little puzzled by this one.

'I thought I knew them all,' he said, surprised.

'Ah, but this is a special one,' said Owen.

'I must look up this Sheikh Abd Al-Samad.'

'Yes, you should do that,' said Owen, 'afterwards.'

The procession, unusually, would be led by the Mufti himself. It was said that he wished to give special emphasis to the day's meaning.

The other unusual feature was that he would be accompanied by the Mamur Zapt.

'Smart wheeze!' said the regulars in the bar, nudging each other knowingly.

'The Pied Piper in person,' said Paul tartly.

The procession set off late in the afternoon when the sun was beginning to go off the streets but its rays could still sparkle redly in the brass-backed mirrors which were an essential part of any procession. It would finish in the dark, when the flaming torches and little red lanterns and fireworks could be seen to best advantage.

Since the Mufti was at its head, the leading ranks were full of the illustrious. These did not include the Widow Shawquat and the barber, who nevertheless were prominent in a second phalanx led by Selim. Beside them, dogged to the last, hobbled the Sheikh Hussein Al-Jamal Abd-el-Assid.

Owen marched beside the Mufti. They had much to talk about, little of which concerned the saintly merits of Abd Al-Samad.

'What an excellent opportunity!' said the Mufti. 'I've been wanting to talk to you for a long time.'

'We must do this more often,' said Owen.

Small boys ran along the fringes of the procession. One such small boy drew up alongside Owen as he was talking to the Mufti.

'Effendi!' hissed Ali. 'He is here!'

'Who?'

'Your rival. What do you advise?'

'Keep walking!' counselled Owen. 'Let him die of sun-stroke.'

Baffled, Ali dropped back.

The Widow Shawquat had dropped back, too. So had the Sheikh Hussein Al-Jamal Abd-el-Assid. A little later, however, Owen saw them again, once more in their position at the head of the second phalanx. This time, though, the Sheikh was sitting in a wheelbarrow, pushed by a stout, but bemused, workman under the close supervision of the Widow Shawquat.

The progress of that part of the procession was a little unsteady because the barber kept stopping, the better to harangue those about him.

Not far away Selim looked nervous. This was not just because the barber had brought his working tools with him and every so often there was the bright flash of scissors in the air. It was because, with the misplaced feeling of responsibility for the universe of the over-conscientious, he was casting around in his mind for things that could go wrong. Owen was relieved to see, a little later, that Barclay had joined him. One man, at least, knew what this was all about.

The procession turned up the broad boulevard between the Ministries. People came out of the buildings and marched in the procession for a short while to show their respects.

Among them, forewarned of the presence of the Mufti and eager to demonstrate the religious zeal which was commonly and so wrongly supposed to be lacking in them, were several Ministers. They fell in naturally beside the Mufti.

'This saint must be important, O Mufti,' they said, 'since you are leading his procession.'

'It is not the man himself,' said the Mufti, 'but what he stands for.'

'Of course! Of course!'

'What does he stand for?' asked the Mufti.

'Well . . .'

'I will tell you,' said the Mufti, and recounted the story of Sheikh Abd Al-Samad.

When he had finished, there was a puzzled silence.

'You said it was what he stood for?' said one of the Ministers hesitantly.

'A Camel of Destruction is about to march through the city,' said the Mufti sternly.

'He is?'

The Mufti looked back over the procession behind him. It stretched out all the way down the boulevard and then bent out of sight down the Sharia el Mobtaddyan. From further away, the Midan Nasriyeh, perhaps, or perhaps even the Place Sayida Zeinab, came the sound of drums which indicated that the tail was still assembling.

'And all these good people are prepared to lie in its way,' said the Mufti. 'There are a lot of them, don't you think? But then, you politicians don't care about numbers.'

The Ministers, mindful of their voters, were not so sure.

'But, Mufti,' said one of them diffidently, 'I still don't see what this Camel is.'

'It is not so much the Camel itself as its path. Which

happens to go in a straight line from the Bab-el-Azab to the Bab-el-Futuh. Right through the Old City with all its mosques. I am sure, gentlemen,' said the Mufti sweetly, 'that you understand now the special significance of our blessed Sheikh.'

CHAPTER 13

The Ministers did understand the significance of the Blessed Sheikh. A day or two later it became known that the road was not going to be proceeded with.

The fact that the Mufti had come out so strongly against the road and the scale of the support had also impressed the British. The word *jihad*, or holy war, was suddenly on people's lips. The Consul-General shook his head and Paul went out among the foreign bankers with a long face muttering the word 'risky'. He did not go into details; simple repetition of the word, which seemed to have awful significance for bankers, was enough.

Support for the project crumbled. The Khedive was furious. What were the British there for, he demanded? If it wasn't to make sure that the banks got their cash, what was it? Why didn't they get on and use those expensive soldiers?

The bankers didn't care to hear it put quite so plainly and war would clash with the Army's Sports Day, so confrontation was postponed.

This suited the Nationalists, except the more militant ones. Unusually, however, they found themselves rallying to the support of the Khedive. Roads were plainly progress. The Khedive, wrong-headed though he was on most things, was right on this. Modernization was what the country needed. The fact that the British were opposing it was surely guarantee enough of its being in the country's interests.

Barclay bought Owen a drink. Even Selim, whom they collected from his work on the little sparkling, blue-tiled mosque, was tempted to join them in it, though in the end he stuck to coffee. He intended, he confided, to go and see Aisha's parents afterwards.

They parted outside the Fingaris' door. As Owen turned away he found Ali watching aghast.

'You are too generous, effendi!' he wailed. 'I know the British say you should give your adversary a sporting chance but this is ridiculous!'

'It's not like that,' said Owen, feeling it incumbent on him to set Ali's overheated mind at rest.

'Well, at least it's not Jabir,' said Ali, when eventually he became reconciled.

Owen caught him by the shoulder.

'What was that you said?'

'You spoke of him yourself, effendi!' cried Ali, alarmed.

'I know I did. What do you know of him?'

'You don't have to worry about him, effendi,' said Ali, rubbing his shoulder. 'Aisha has already rejected him.'

'I know that,' said Owen, 'but how do you?'

'I heard her rebuff him, effendi. He went to her house. She would not even give him admittance. But he is a nasty man, effendi. Afterwards he went back and spoke with her brother. "I will have her," he said, "one way or another. You go back and command her." "She does not love you," Osman said. "What has that got to do with it?" asked Jabir. "You are her brother. She is yours to command." "She will not," said Osman. "You see she does," said Jabir, "or you know what will happen."'

'How did you hear all this?'

'I happened to be standing by,' said Ali. 'They sat outside at a café.'

'Did you think Jabir might wish to use you?'

'Effendi!' said Ali, shocked. 'How could you think a thing like that!'

'Has he used you before?'

'Effendi! Well, perhaps occasionally.'

'With Aisha?'

'She would not receive his letters. Afterwards, he would blame me and beat me. So I refused to take them. Well, until he offered me more money. Effendi—'

'Yes?'

'It was not the beating that I minded but the way he did the beating.'

'What way was that?'

'As one might beat a dog if one especially wished to hurt it.'

'I understand.'

'I think Aisha did, too, and that is why she would not have him.'

'That day, when he spoke with Osman, what else did he say?'

'I could not understand. They spoke in riddles.'

'Did you learn what it was that Jabir threatened?'

'No, effendi. But Osman protested and said they were two different things. And Jabir said that to him they were the same, and that if Osman did not do them both he would betray him. And Osman said he could do the other thing but not this thing, and that this thing was small and the other big. But Jabir said that this thing was big to him and he would have it so.'

'And then?'

'Jabir left.'

'And Osman?'

'He put his head on his arms and wept.'

'Anything I can do to help,' murmured Jabir politely. 'Where shall we start?'

'How about when you first met up with him again after

he had left College? You were working for a bank then, I believe?'

'In a manner of speaking, yes.'

'The Trans-Levant. Which concerned itself largely with property speculation.'

'Investment,' said Jabir, 'investment.'

'And Osman Fingari had just been appointed to the Ministry of Public Works. Which was very convenient.'

Jabir looked at him warily.

'Was it?'

'Yes. He was responsible for planning matters in the part of Cairo in which you were interested.'

'We have interests everywhere.'

'The Bab-el-Azab. Did you approach him over that, I wonder?'

'I don't think so. I certainly don't remember doing so.'

'That is strange, because the Trans-Levant was buying up property in that area and seeking permission to develop.'

'Ah, but that would have been someone else.'

'You didn't approach Osman Fingari to, let us say, make things easier?'

'I wasn't involved in that project at all.'

'That, too, is strange, for someone who knows you, remembers you as active in it, too.'

'Not very active.'

'Very active,' said Owen, 'or so this person says.'

Jabir shrugged.

'Be that so or not,' said Owen, 'the application was approved. By Osman Fingari.'

Jabir shrugged again.

'And this is where I'm hoping you will be able to help me: was the Bab-el-Azab project before Tufa or after?'

'Tufa?' said Jabir.

'You remember Tufa? It was a question of enclosing land from the desert, at a nominal price because it was to be used for industrial development. Again you approached Fingari, and again he approved.'

'I don't remember approaching him. We handle a lot of projects.'

'You might remember this one, because you approached him again. After he had moved to the Ministry of Agriculture. This time it was over registering a change of land use.'

'I believe I recall something now. Wasn't it to do with water?'

'I am so glad you remember. You see, there is a record of your presence at a meeting where the application was discussed.'

Jabir smiled. 'Are you not making a mystery of something innocuous, Captain Owen?'

'Is financial deception innocuous, Mr Sabry?'

'All businessmen try it on, Captain Owen. That is all I plead guilty to.'

'Ah, but look at it from the other point of view, Osman Fingari's. There are rules in such matters for public servants.'

'The most he could be condemned for is the indulgence of a friend.'

'Not quite the most. Did not money change hands?'

'You would have to prove that, Captain Owen.'

'More to the point, you could, if required.'

'I don't quite follow you.'

'Was not that the object? To put Osman Fingari in a blackmailable position? So as to be sure he would do as he was told.'

'You've lost me, I'm afraid.'

'You wanted his connivance over something rather bigger: the deal with the Agricultural Bank.'

'You make me sound very sinister, Captain Owen.'

'I think you are sinister, Mr Sabry. You very deliberately set about catching your friend in the meshes of a carefully prepared net. You trapped him over Tufa and I suspect that when we have finished our investigations we shall find that you trapped him over Bab-el-Azab, too. And this was done so that you could wedge him in over the deal with the Agricultural Bank. But that, actually, is not the worst of it.'

'No?'

'No. Having trapped him, you tightened the screw, and you did that not because it was necessary but because you wanted to.'

'He was dragging his feet.'

'A little. Others were pressuring him, too. But that does not explain why you deliberately did it to the point when he broke.'

'Everyone puts pressure on.'

'But not everyone enjoys pressing to the point of destruction.'

'How was I to know he would commit suicide?'

'Because you knew he had nearly done it before. You knew Osman well, Mr Sabry. You knew how weak he was and the extent of your own influence over him. You had tormented him at school and you had enjoyed the torment-ing. When the chance came again, you enjoyed that. He was your bird, Mr Sabry.'

'Bird?'

'Don't you remember the incident of the bird from your schooldays? It had a damaged wing and your schoolfriends urged you to kill it. So you did, but not quickly.'

'I don't know what you're talking about.'

'Was Aisha going to be your bird, too, Mr Sabry?'

'Aisha!'

'I think she was, only she knew it and would not have you.'

'What has Aisha got to do with it?'

'When she rebuffed you, it made you ugly inside. You had to work that out of you. You went back to Osman. You knew he was there and trapped and that you could do what you liked with him. You tightened the screw until he screamed and then tightened it again. He screamed again and then you tightened again. And then he died.'

'I didn't mean to kill him,' said Jabir hoarsely.

'I think once you had started tightening and he had started screaming you could not stop,' said Owen.

'He had, you see, two agendas,' he explained; 'the one set by his employers and his own. His employers admit the pressure but say, naturally, that it was never intended to go so far. When he gave the last twists he was acting on his own.'

'Because that was the kind of guy he was?'

'Exactly.'

'You'll never convict him,' said Georgiades positively. 'Pressure isn't a crime.'

'Blackmail is. Offering inducements is. I'll get him on those.'

'Will you be able to prove it?'

'You'd be surprised,' said Owen drily, 'how cooperative his employers are. So anxious are they to dissociate themselves from Jabir's acts that they are providing me with all sorts of details about his activities.'

'Who *were* his employers?' asked Georgiades.

'There were several groups interested in the deal going ahead.'

'The Agricultural Bank?' suggested Georgiades.

'Yes, but Jabir didn't actually work for them directly. Nor, incidentally, did he work for the Khedivial Agricultural Society, which was also interested in the deal going ahead. But he did work for interests outside the Society, a small group whose leader was Ali Reza Pasha. Ali Reza had excellent contacts with Ministers—and so was able to arrange Osman Fingari's transfer—which was probably why the Trans-Levant secured him as an ally. They worked together on the deal and Jabir was the go-between.'

'The Trans-Levant, then.'

'Yes, but it, too, was acting as an agent. Behind it there was a big international bank which sniffed opportunities in Egypt. What it was really interested in was the deal with the Agricultural Bank. It wasn't fussy, though. It was also attracted by the prospect of financing the road. It hesitated between the two. The extra deal on the new seed tipped the balance in favour of the Agricultural Bank. Then when that looked like falling through, it swung the other way.'

'So there *was* a degree of urgency over the deal,' said Georgiades.

'Yes. And I think Fingari knew it could swing the other way and was trying to hold on until it did. He was a Nationalist, you see. He was suspicious of the Agricultural deal because he thought it would be at the expense of the fellahin. On the other hand he was in favour of the road because, well, that was modernization, that was progress.'

'So he wasn't just venal?'

'Oh no, he had his ideals, too.'

Georgiades hesitated.

'I think I would tell Aisha that,' he said.

A thing then happened which was to Owen, still, obviously, innocent in the ways of the financial world, surprising. The deal on the road having fallen through, the big international bank announced that it was once more interested in lending to the Agricultural Bank.

'You're not going to let it go ahead, are you?' said Owen, outraged.

'Oh yes,' said Paul, 'and tap it for some more if we can. Lenders are scarcer than borrowers. Especially in Egypt just at the moment.'

Paul was now reconciled to Owen, having heard that the sum he had raised from the Khedivial Agricultural Society had been paid straight into the Public Accounts and that the Head of Audit had personally approved the large transfer into Owen's hospitality budget which had made possible his convivial evening at the opera.

Nikos went into a state of deep shock.

Yussuf was overjoyed and went to the Agricultural Bank as soon as it resumed lending. On his way home, however, Satan tempted him and he determined to divorce his existing wife and embark on a more stirring existence with someone younger. As soon as he reached home he informed his wife, in accordance with Islamic law, that she was henceforth divorced.

'Oh, am I?' she said. 'In that case you had better pay me back my dowry,' fairly confident that he could not.

'Here it is,' said Yussuf, counting out seven pounds from the money he had just received.

He then approached the father of an attractive girl he had seen.

'A bit out of your reach,' the father said. 'Her dowry is twelve pounds.'

'Only twelve-pounds?' and Yussuf counted it out.

When he asked his new bride to let him have back the £12 so that he could buy seed, she refused, knowing that he had divorced his first wife and guessing that he would soon tire of her.

Sure enough, it was not long before he was regretting his decision. He divorced his new wife and went back to his old one and asked her to marry him again.

'Very well,' she said, 'but now you owe me five pounds. Her dowry was twelve pounds and mine was only seven pounds.'

'All right,' said Yussuf and let her have the £5, which was, as it happened, all that he had left of the sum he had borrowed from the Agricultural Bank.

Both wives then lent out their money locally at a handsome rate of interest. They were not alone. A surprising number of fellahin had gone down the same slippery path as Yussuf.

The result was a considerable transfer of wealth from the fellahin to their wives. Not long after, it was estimated that the fellahin women had become creditors to three-fifths of the debts of the fellahin. The Agricultural Bank was a poor second.

Which left Owen even more puzzled about the ways of the financial world.

He himself, however, had his own difficulties.

'*Still* no money?' said Zeinab's father, Nuri Pasha, affecting surprise. 'With all your opportunities? What *have* you been doing?'